"You said you'd leave me alone."

Rohan's eyebrows rose. "I said I'd transfer my attentions where they'd be appreciated." He paused meaningfully. "I think your daughter appreciates them, don't you? Words are your *metier*, Cass. Didn't your trained ear tell you I was being slightly ambiguous in what I said?"

"No! Obviously I underestimated you—yet again. Well, I don't want Jodie to think these outings are going to be a regular occurrence." Cass rounded on him. "And we don't need your amateur psychology either. If you feel Jodie is lacking men's company, then I'll do something about it. I don't need your interference."

"Don't tempt me to tell you what you do need." Rohan's voice was soft, but the glance which raked her was insinuating.

She'd been out-maneuvered, she realized angrily. And now it was two against one!

SARA CRAVEN writes consistently strong stories, which makes her one of our most popular writers in the Harlequin Presents line. With her fresh approach and polished style, she is a constant delight to romance readers everywhere.

Books by Sara Craven

HARLEQUIN PRESENTS
704—DARK PARADISE
815—ALIEN VENGEANCE
832—ACT OF BETRAYAL
856—PROMISE OF THE UNICORN
872—ESCAPE ME NEVER

HARLEQUIN ROMANCE
1943—THE GARDEN OF DREAMS

These books may be available at your local bookseller.

Don't miss any of our special offers. Write to us at the following address for information on our newest releases.

Harlequin Reader Service
901 Fuhrmann Blvd.
P.O. Box 1325, Buffalo, NY 14269
Canadian address: P.O. Box 2800, Postal Station A,
5170 Yonge St., Willowdale, Ont. M2N 6J3

SARA CRAVEN

escape me never

Harlequin Books

TORONTO • NEW YORK • LONDON
AMSTERDAM • PARIS • SYDNEY • HAMBURG
STOCKHOLM • ATHENS • TOKYO • MILAN

Harlequin Presents first edition April 1986
ISBN 0-373-10872-9

Original hardcover edition published in 1985
by Mills & Boon Limited

CHAPTER ONE

IT had begun to rain. Cassie felt the first icy drops, as she waited on the edge of the pavement, and grimaced inwardly with irritation. She'd left the flat so hurriedly that morning that she'd failed to bring either an umbrella or even a scarf, and a heavy shower on her newly washed, carefully blow-dried and disciplined hair was likely to restore it to its usual riot of tumbling waves.

Clearly, it was going to be one of those days. Her radio alarm had gone off early, tempting her to the luxury of 'just a few more minutes', with the result that she'd fallen deeply asleep again.

And Jodie, usually the most amenable of children, had suddenly exhibited disturbing signs of a reversion to the panicky, hysterical tempers of a few years previously.

'You haven't forgotten it's open afternoon at school, Mummy,' she said, as Cassie dashed between toaster and kettle. 'Miss Willard asked specially if you were going to be there.'

Cassie concealed her dismay at the reminder. Yes, it had slipped her mind, like so many other things did these days, she thought glumly, resentment rising within her at Jodie's reference to her headmistress. Her school was well-run, and briskly geared to learning, but Miss Willard whose old-fashioned values oiled the wheels, had what amounted to an obsession with working mothers, holding them, Cassie often thought, responsible for most of the ills plaguing modern society.

And the fact that Cassie was a widow and needed to support herself and her child apparently made no difference to her views. She had never made the slightest allowance for women who worked, scheduling most school functions during normal job hours, and taking careful note, Cassie thought ruefully, of those who coped with awkwardness and inconvenience to be there. It was moral blackmail, and although Cassie, and others in the same boat as herself might grumble at it, none of them would have dreamed of removing their children from the school itself.

Now, with Jodie, Cassie sought to temporise. 'I'll try, darling,' she promised. 'But it's a very big day at the office. But Mrs Barrett will be there,' she added reassuringly.

Besides the stability of school, Mrs Barrett was the other blessing in their lives. A comfortable, motherly soul whose family had grown up, and who was happy to fill in the years before one of her own brood made her a grandmother by looking after Jodie on a more or less full-time basis.

It couldn't have been more convenient. She lived in the flat below, and took Jodie to school each morning, as well as bringing her home in the afternoons, giving her tea, and playing with her until Cassie arrived home. She was well-paid, of course, but she never treated Jodie as if she was a source of income.

Now, to Cassie's horror, she saw her daughter's lip bulge ominously. 'I don't want Mrs Barrett,' she said tremulously. 'I want *you* to be there like the other mummies. You didn't come to the carol concert, and I was the only one in our class,' she added, her voice rising perilously.

She was beginning to stiffen. Cassie, biting her lip, knelt beside her, putting her arms round the rigid little body. 'Sweetheart,' she said gently. 'It isn't that easy. We've discussed all this before. I have to work to earn money for us to live on, you know that.'

'We could have a Daddy to do that,' Jodie said sullenly. 'Proper families have daddies.' And her eyes met Cassie's, suddenly, shockingly Brett's eyes.

Cassie bit her lip hard. Thank you, Miss Willard, she thought grimly. The school had a lot to its credit, but on the debit side was this constant reinforcement of the traditional stereotyped roles for the sexes, the insistence of the nuclear family as the norm, isolating those children whose lives did not conform to the cosy pattern. Making them aware that they were somehow different.

She had never felt less humorous in her life, but she tried to make a joke of it. 'Well, daddies don't grow on trees, I'm afraid, and neither does money.' She got up. 'I'll do my very best to be there this afternoon. What time does it start—three o'clock, as usual?'

Jodie nodded slowly, her eyes wide and anxious fixed on her mother's face, but that alarming stiffness was beginning to subside. And in a way, Cass thought, it might even be a hopeful sign, after all that had happened, that she could talk about fathers, although in general terms. It was one of those moments she ought to pursue, to build on, and she knew it both for Jodie's sake and her own, and for a moment she was tempted to 'phone in to the office and tell them she wouldn't be in.

But she couldn't do it, she told herself reluctantly. Today was too important for the agency. They hadn't exactly been in the doldrums recently, but the *Eve* cosmetics account would be a magnificent boost—a real feather in their caps if its board liked the advertising campaign they had designed, and which would get its initial presentation that morning.

There shouldn't be any snags. The ideas were there, and they were good. Even Barney, their boss, thought so. Now, all they had to do was sell it to the clients. That, thankfully, wasn't her job. Roger was always the front man on these occasions, enthusiastic, persuasive, a born salesman. They made a good team.

And if they secured the *Eve* cosmetics account, there'd been broad hints that other goodies from Grant International might be coming their way. The sky, in fact, was the limit.

If things went well, it could all be over by lunchtime, she told herself optimistically. And Roger would let her leave early. In the general euphoria, Barney might not even notice her absence. In his way, he was a male Miss Willard, also prepared to make no concessions, as he'd warned Cass when he hired her.

'Women with small children are generally bad news,' he'd told her brusquely. 'Here,—er Ms Linton—the job comes first.' He gave her a faint glare. 'Not measles, or half term, or whatever. I don't want there to be any misunderstanding. There'll be no special favours.'

Well, there hadn't been, nor had she ever asked for any. But in spite of Mrs Barrett's unfailing willingness to be her substitute, Cass had not always found it easy.

And being late, as she was bound to be today of all days, wouldn't do her cause any particular good.

But her lateness wasn't actually noticed. The agency was buzzing, nobody in their offices and studios. Sylvie, with whom Cass shared an office, was on the 'phone talking agitatedly as Cass came in, and she waved a hand at her, rolling her eyes to heaven as she did so.

'Phew.' She almost slung the receiver back on its rest, and leaned back in her chair. 'Which do you want first—the bad news or the bad news?'

'Oh, God.' Cass sat down at her desk. 'Don't tell me—they're not coming.'

'They're coming all right, but they'll be delayed.'

Cass's heart sank. 'But why?'

'They're waiting for the new chairman to fly in from Paris. It seems he likes to be in on every act, and they don't know what's hit them.' Sylvie paused. 'And Roger's wife's been on the 'phone. He's in bed with 'flu—temperature up in the hundreds, and the doctor's forbidden him to move.'

'Oh, I don't believe it,' Cass said limply. 'He was complaining of a headache last night, but I thought—well, you know what I thought . . .'

Sylvie nodded. Apart from his job and his family, Roger's other prevailing interest was his health. He enjoyed a mild but persistent hypochondria which his colleagues either tolerated or fumed over, according to temperament.

'One of his little Wednesday moans,' she agreed. 'But this time it's for real. And Barney's bellowing like a wounded bull,' she added grimly. 'And that's nothing to the way he'll react when he sees what you're wearing. Hell, Cassie, you know how he feels about women wearing trousers to work.'

Cass flushed. 'And you know how I feel about his stupid chauvinist prejudices about clothes,' she retorted with energy. 'Besides what does it matter. I'm the backroom girl.'

'Not today, sweetie,' Sylvie reminded her acidly. 'Roger's demolishing the nation's stock of soluble aspirin—remember? So you'll have to do the presentation.'

'What?' Cass's face was appalled. 'Sylvie—I can't.'

'You're going to have to,' Sylvie said unsympathetically. 'For heaven's sake, ninety per cent of the ideas in the campaign are yours, anyway. And you've heard Roger do presentations dozens of times. Just sock it to them, like he does.'

Cass said flatly, 'It's impossible. I'm not Roger, and you know it.'

'You're certainly healthier,' Sylvie agreed cheerfully. 'But there's no reason why you shouldn't speak up for yourself for once. Old Roger may have the gift of the gab, but you do most of the work, and everyone knows it. You carry him, Cass.'

Cass's lips parted in further protest, but before she could utter another word, the door of the office burst open and Barney erupted into the room, calling something to someone over his shoulder as he came.

His glance flashed to Cass. 'So you finally got here,' he said.

'Yes,' Cass said non-committally, reflecting bitterly that there wasn't a lot that ever got past Barney.

'Damn Roger,' he went on forcefully. 'Three hundred and sixty four other days he could have had 'flu, but he has to pick this one. The presentation—you can cope.' It was a statement rather than a question. 'Well, you'll have to. I'll back you up, of course, but the thing's your pigeon.' He gave her a long assessing look, and sighed. 'And for God's sake do something to yourself before they get here.'

Cass straightened, and her eyes flashed fire. 'What's the matter with the way I look?'

'Nothing—if sludge and leaf-mould are your favourite colours,' Barney said disagreeably. 'And you're trying to sell a cosmetics campaign, not promote the well-scrubbed look. Don't you think it might have been tactful to have worn some of their stuff?'

Sylvie said, 'If you'll excuse me,' and slid out of the room. Neither of them saw her go.

Cass almost bounced out of her chair. 'I thought you'd hired me for my brains. If you wanted a glamour girl, you should have gone elsewhere,' she flared.

'I would have—no danger,' Barney threw back at her. He discovered a new bone of contention. 'Trousers,' he howled. 'Christ, today of all days couldn't you have sacrificed your bloody feminist principles and worn a skirt?'

It had nothing to do with feminist principles, but was the result of laddering her last pair of tights during that maddening early rush, but she wasn't going to give him the satisfaction of telling him so.

'I'll wear what I want, and if you don't like it you can fire me,' she hurled at him recklessly. 'You took me on for what was inside my head, not for any half inch of muck plastered on my face.' She banged a fist on the table. 'This is how I am, and you can take it or leave it.'

There was a silence, then slowly she saw his face crinkle into a reluctant smile, like the sun emerging from behind a thunder-cloud. 'I'll take you, Cass,' he said. 'Warts and all. You're the best ideas girl this agency's had in years. If we get this account, it will be down to you basically, and I won't forget it. It's just ...' He paused. 'Hell, the clients expect an image from you, as well as the campaign. Usually, you have Roger to hide behind, but you won't today and—well, it is important.'

Cass looked back at him with the beginnings of ruefulness. 'I know it,' she acknowledged quietly. 'And—I promise I'll do my best, but I can't change the kind of person I am.'

'No-one's asking you to,' Barney assured her. 'But—look, Cass, they're going to be late as it is, waiting for their latest big shot to join them You've got time to pop out—get yourself something else to wear. The agency will pay, naturally.'

Cass sighed. 'What do you suggest?' she asked bitterly. 'Something short and see-through? I'm sorry, Barney, but I just can't. It would be false to everything I've come to believe in.' She bit her lip. 'After all, if I was Roger, you wouldn't be in here criticising the tie I'd chosen, or my aftershave. Why should it be different, just because I happen to be a woman?'

Barney gave her one of his deliberately disarming looks, usually saved for clients with grievances. 'That's the million dollar question, Cass, but there is a difference, and it will take a few more generations of women's liberation to remove it. Well, have it your own way,' he added briskly. 'And at least your hair looks better for once,' he added as he headed for the door again. 'What have you done to it.'

Cass said without rancour, 'I got it caught in the rain.'

When she was alone, she sat down slowly, resting her elbows on the desk, and cupping her chin reflectively in her hands. What Barney and everyone else at the agency didn't know was that there'd once been a Cass Linton who'd been as fashion conscious as anyone else, who'd enjoyed enhancing her natural attractions with make-up and scent. But that girl was long since dead, and the new personality which had risen painfully from the ashes of the old preferred to camouflage herself in drab clothes, and severe hairstyles. She didn't want people to look at her as they once had. She didn't want, in particular, men to look at her. She was a widow. She wanted no other relationship in her life, and although she no longer wore Brett's ring, she carried it with her always to remind her.

She examined her hands judiciously. Bare, with neat unpolished nails. A neat face too, pale-lipped and unremarkable, her clear blue-green eyes its chief beauty. And—neat hair, when the wind and rain hadn't played havoc with it, turning it into a dark curling mop instead of the usual controlled bob. Everything about her designed so that people wouldn't give her a second look.

But today, whether she liked it or not, everyone would be looking, and making judgments, and the thought irritated her almost unbearably. She'd made unobtrusiveness her leitmotif, and today, through no fault of her own, she was going to be the centre of attention.

It might not be so bad, she tried to console herself. After all, executives from the *Eve* cosmetics board had visited the agency on a number of occasions. Only the new chairman, the overlord of Grant Industries, was an unknown quantity.

She tried briefly to review what little she knew about him, culled mainly from agency gossip. Quite young, she'd gathered, for the onerous position he now occupied after his father's retirement. Had spent a lot of time in the States, but for the past couple of years had been European director. Was expected to take a firm hold on Grant's worldwide business interests, but had not, frankly, been expected to interest himself in a relatively minor detail like an advertising promotion for Eve Cosmetics.

No wonder Barney was going off like a firecracker, jumping in all directions, Cass thought wrily. She could have coped adequately with Mr McDowell, and Mr Handson. But Rohan Grant was additional pressure which she could have well done without.

Sylvie popped her head round the door. 'Is it safe to come back?' she asked. 'What have you done with the body?'

'The body's alive and well, and no doubt playing hell somewhere else,' Cass said, with a faint grin.

'And you're sticking to your guns?' Sylvie asked.

'Why not?'

'Oh.' Sylvie hunched a shoulder. 'I thought you might have—compromised for once. Under the circumstances.'

Cass looked at her in mild surprise. 'But I thought you agreed with me,' she said. 'Barney's blatant sexism has always infuriated you too.'

'Yes,' Sylvie agreed. 'Although his wife seems to thrive on it,' she added drily. 'At the last Christmas party she told me she'd gone back into stockings and suspenders because he preferred them.'

'Well, good luck to her,' Cass said, shrugging. 'I hope you're not suggesting I should do the same to woo Rohan Grant and his cohorts.'

'No, that would be going too far.' Sylvie hesitated. 'Oh, what's the use in pretending. Bloody Barney wants me to persuade you out of those khaki horrors you're smothered in, and into something with a skirt. And for once, I see his point,' she added hastily as Cass opened her mouth to protest. 'Whether you want it or not, today you're the agency's spokesperson. They're going to judge us all by you, or at least Rohan Grant will. You know how important the right impression can be,' she went on appealingly. 'Cass, I feel a total heel saying these things to you, but just for once, can't you forget your aim of fading into the wallpaper—and look the successful lady you are?'

There was a silence. Cass said, 'Quite a speech. What do you want me to do? Take Barney's thirty pieces of silver and get myself a basic black?' Her tone was bitter.

'Why not?' Sylvie's voice was equable. 'You've got a part to play, so dress up for it. It might even make it easier.'

Cass bit her lip. 'That—actually makes sense,' she admitted slowly. 'All right—I'll do it, for this occasion only. Did Barney give you any further instructions?'

Sylvie giggled. 'Can you doubt it? He said we were to get something which matched your eyes and showed off your legs.' She sent Cass a droll look. 'So much for Operation Chameleon.'

And after a stunned moment, Cass found herself joining helplessly in her laughter.

But two hours later, she had stopped smiling. The clients still hadn't arrived, and any remaining hope she'd had of getting off for Jodie's open day was vanishing fast.

She sighed irritably. The day was proving a chapter of disasters from start to finish, and this—charade she'd allowed Sylvie to talk her into it, was one of the worst. The dress, a simple cream wool sheath with a cowl neck, was the most expensive garment she'd ever possessed, but she took no pleasure in it, or in the broad leather belt which cinched her waist, reducing its slenderness almost to nothing, or the matching dark brown shoes, the heels of which added over an inch to her height. And to add insult to injury, Sylvie had produced one of the *Eve* cosmetic beauty cases, and insisted on Cass touching her eyelids with a delicate tracing of pearly shadow, and smoothing a soft pink gloss on to the indignant lines of her mouth.

Sylvie, she thought sourly, seemed well pleased with her handiwork. 'It's like one of those old Hollywood movies,' she'd said, grinning. 'All we need now is for Barney to come in and say, "My God, Ms Linton—but you're beautiful."'

'I'm glad you think it's so damned funny,' Cass had snapped back.

Perhaps Sylvie had warned Barney to step warily, for all he said in the event was a quiet, 'Thanks, Cassie.'

No one else made any comment at all. But that, Cass thought caustically, was probably because they didn't recognise her. To tell the truth, she hardly recognised herself. And the reflection which looked back at her from the mirror was hardly a reassuring one. It was too powerful a reminder of the vulnerable girl she had been, rather than the guarded self-sufficient woman which marriage, and the subsequent bringing up of her child as a single parent, had made her. She didn't want to remember that girl, or any of the circumstances which had brought about that change in her.

She ran an irritable hand through her hair. Allowed to go its own way like this, it made her look years younger. Oh, she would be so thankful when this day was over, and she could retire back into her inconspicuous shell again.

She opened the door of the women's cloakroom

and hurried into the corridor, colliding as she did so with the leading figure in a group of people just walking past.

For a startled instant, she was off-balance, sharply aware of muscular strength, and a cool, clean male scent. Then firm hands took her shoulders, steadying her, and she recoiled with a gasp.

She heard Barney say jovially, 'Cass—I've just sent Linda to find you and tell you that we're on our way to the board room now. May I introduce Rohan Grant to you. Mr Grant, this is Ms Linton who will be conducting the presentation of the campaign on our behalf today.'

A man's voice drawling slightly said, 'If I've left her any breath to do it with. How do you do, Ms Linton.'

She looked at him almost dazedly, registering all kinds of things. His height, for one thing. He seemed to tower head and shoulders above anyone else in the group. His superbly cut suit accentuated the breadth of his shoulders, and the lean hips and long legs. A thin, tanned face, with nose and chin strongly and commandingly marked, and a firm, straight mouth. Long-lashed hazel eyes glinting with amusement, and something else, and brown hair curling away from his forehead.

It was as if she was making notes for an inventory. She swallowed. There was no actual facial resemblance between them, but Brett's hair had been brown and his eyes hazel. And there was a terrible familiarity in that arrogant lift of the head, that unspoken assumption that he was male—all powerful, and all conquering . . . All so like Brett, she thought with a kind of sick horror.

Barney said sharply, 'Cass, are you all right?'

She dredged up some self-control from somewhere. She said coolly, 'Fine, thank you. I'll join you in the board room right away. She moved her lips in a brief meaningless smile. 'Mr Grant—gentlemen.'

Her office was empty, and she was thankful. All the material for the presentation had already been set up in the boardroom. There was only her personal folder of notes to take. She reached for it, aware that her hand was shaking a little, and her breathing ragged.

She had to get a grip on herself, she told herself sternly. There were thousands of brownhaired, hazel-eyed men in the Greater London area alone. She saw them every day on the streets, in the Tube, in the restaurants around the office. And he didn't look like Brett, she reminded herself almost frantically. It was the colouring only—and the stance which made her think . . .

But she couldn't forget that for a brief moment she had touched him. And he had touched her. She had actually felt the warmth of his hands on her through the fabric of her dress. She shuddered violently. The first time—the first time a man had touched her, apart from cursory, unavoidable handshakes, since Brett's death.

And it was no use telling herself that it was her own fault, that she'd crashed into him purely accidentally. Just that one fleeting contact, and she felt threatened.

She wanted to run away, to hide somewhere. But there was nowhere. And they were waiting for her. At any minute, Barney would be sending

someone to hurry her up. She was needed to do
her job, the job which paid the rent and
supported not just herself, but her child. The job
she couldn't afford to lose by keeping important
clients waiting while she stayed, shivering, in her
room. She must have scored zero for poise with
the Grant man already. She couldn't compound
the bad impression. She snatched up the folder,
and her bag, then paused again.

Obeying an impulse she barely understood, she
opened her bag and unzipped a small inside
pocket, and took out Brett's ring, biting at the
inside of her lip, as she forced it over her knuckle.
Her hands had grown a little. The ring felt tight,
alien on her finger.

She had never thought to wear it again, had
kept it solely as a private reminder of her
marriage, but now, suddenly, it seemed like the
safeguard she needed and had abandoned with
her shapeless khaki trousers and jacket.

But why should she suddenly be so sure she
needed a safeguard? That was the question that
followed her, tormenting her, all down the long
corridor to the board room where they all waited.

CHAPTER TWO

'THE problem we've had to face,' Cass said, her voice clear and even, 'has been the old one of familiarity breeding contempt. Everyone knows Eve cosmetics. The range is as established and respected as Arden or Rubenstein. Yet in spite of everything that's been done to make sure the products moved with the times, this frankly hasn't been reflected in your advertising campaigns over the past ten years, nor by the sales. Your non-allergic brands—the fact that you've produced a whole range without using animal products—all these things should have been exploited—but haven't been.'

She paused. 'The ideas we've put to you seek to put this right, and also to hammer home the message of the brand name. *Eve* is all woman, and *Eve* cosmetics are designed for all women.'

She smiled briefly and sat down, amid appreciative murmurs. But were they really enthusiastic, or merely polite. Cass couldn't gauge any more. She felt as if she'd been put through a wringer, mentally as well as physically.

And Roger enjoyed this, she thought limply. How could he, but she knew what the answer to that was. If Roger had been here, the line of questioning would have been very different. It would have been taken for granted that Roger knew his job, because he was a man. As a woman, Cass had had to prove she knew what she was talking about over and over again. And the man heading the Inquisition had been Rohan Grant.

At first his questions had bewildered her a little, and she'd begun to flounder. Then she caught Barney's warning glance, and realised that she was being tested. She resented this, and it put her on her mettle. She believed in the product—if women had to wear make-up, then *Eve* cosmetics were as good as any and better than most and she believed in the campaign which she'd been instrumental in designing. And if Rohan Grant was used to high-powered performances from bigger agencies, then that was just too bad.

Now, he said, 'Very interesting, Ms Linton, but isn't the image you're trying to create a little—low-key?'

Cass shook her head, 'I don't think so. Whatever the situation may be on the other side of the Atlantic, I don't think women in this country go for the hard sell over anything as personal as make-up and scent. The appeal has to be to the individual, and we have to intrigue her sufficiently to get her into the store, and up to the counter.' She ventured another smile, this time at Mr McDowell. 'The sad fact is that a lot of women feel intimidated by beauty counters. The choice is too vast, and the whole concept of being beautiful rather overwhelming. I want this campaign to interest them so much that they won't just grab the first jar or bottle they see, but ask for *Eve* by name.'

'And are you—overwhelmed by the concept of beauty, Ms Linton?' Rohan Grant asked smoothly. 'I notice you wear the barest minimum of make-up yourself.'

'How very observant of you, Mr Grant,' Cass said calmly. 'And does your eagle eye also tell you what that minimum consists of?'

'Why, yes,' he drawled. 'You're wearing *Silver Jade* shadow, and *Rose Blush* on your lips. But no scent,' he added reflectively. 'I understood sample bottles of both our new fragrances, *Sundance* and *Moonglow* had been sent here.'

'They have.' Cass shrugged slightly. 'They—don't happen to be to my particular taste, I'm afraid.'

He smiled, leaning back in his chair, the hazel eyes surveying her from head to foot with smiling insolence. '*Eve* cosmetics,' he murmured. 'Designed to appeal to all women—except Ms Linton, it seems.'

'Perhaps,' Cass said coolly. 'But that does not mean I don't know how to persuade other women to like them—Mr Grant. I never allow my personal judgments to get in the way of work,' she added sweetly.

'Don't you, Ms Linton?' It was his turn to shrug. 'Well, you'll have a chance to prove that to the hilt in the weeks ahead. We'll give your campaign a trial, and see how it works out.'

She swallowed, managed a feeble, 'Thank you,' and began to gather her papers together. She could sense the jubilation in the air around her, but seemed to have no part in it. She'd been walking the high wire for too long. Rohan Grant's almost laconic bestowal of the account, whether it was on trial or not, could only be an anti-climax. And a glance at her watch revealed that even if she could slip away now, she would be too late for Jodie's open day. She felt weary to death suddenly.

And, of course, there was going to be no chance to slip away. An elaborate cold buffet had been laid out in the next room, and champagne was being poured.

'Honey babe, you were sensational,' Barney whispered, as he pushed a glass into her nerveless hand. He gave her a wicked leer. 'I don't know whether it was your arguments which turned the balance, or those fabulous legs of yours.'

'Thanks,' Cass said drily, not knowing whether to laugh or cry.

'But you had me worried a couple of times,' he went on. 'I had no idea you liked living dangerously. However—it paid off in the end. Expect a big bonus from grateful Uncle Barney.'

'Thanks,' she said again, this time with real gratitude. Barney might make her grind her teeth a lot of the time, but he was unfailingly generous when rewards were called for. She might be able to afford to have some redecoration done—or to take Jodie abroad for a couple of weeks later in the year. It had been a tough winter, with Jodie succumbing, it seemed, to one virus after another, although Cass herself had escaped unscathed. Some Mediterranean sun might be what they both needed.

She put down her untouched glass, and looked for an unobtrusive exit, but her way was blocked.

'Not leaving already, Ms Linton,' Rohan Grant said pleasantly. 'Or may I copy Barney Finiston and call you Cassie? After all, we shall be seeing quite a lot of each other in the coming months.'

Cass looked past him. 'I doubt that, Mr Grant. I'm sure you have far more pressing concerns in your empire than *Eve* cosmetics.'

'Most of my empire, as you call it, seems to be flourishing,' he said drily. 'Which gives me more time to spend on the ailing sections of it, like *Eve*.' He paused. 'It happens to be rather close to my heart. Would you like to know why?'

'Not unless I can use it in one of my campaigns, Mr Grant.' She met his gaze fully for the first time. 'Otherwise it's not really any of my business. Now, perhaps you'll excuse me. I think Barney—Mr Finiston—wants to speak to you.'

His mouth twisted slightly. 'He probably does at that. However there are still several points from today's presentation I would like to go over with you—perhaps over dinner tonight?'

Cass's jaw dropped. She said stupidly, 'I don't understand.'

He looked faintly amused. 'What's so baffling? You eat, I presume, and you've heard of dinner— a meal, consisting of several courses, taken in the evening.'

His tone flicked her on the raw. 'I do seem to recognise it,' she said coolly. 'But I'm afraid I have other plans.'

'Change them,' he suggested. His voice was pleasant, but the note of command was implicit, and unmistakable.

'I'll do nothing of the sort,' Cass said, her voice shaking a little. 'Incredible as it may seem, Mr Grant, I have no wish to have dinner with you tonight, or any other evening. And if the *Eve* account is conditional on my agreement, you'd better say so now. I think Barney might have something to say about a member of his staff being—sexually harrassed even by an important client like you.'

She paused. 'And in case you hadn't noticed, I happen to be married.'

He gave her a long, hard look. She'd made him, she thought detachedly, very angry.

'I'd like to meet your husband,' he said silkily at last. 'He must have the guts of Genghis Khan to get to first base with you, you little fire eater. The invitation, as it happens, was to dinner, not to bed. Christ, woman, I thought the next round of discussions could take place in slightly more congenial surroundings, that's all. A table is often more conducive to agreement being reached than a desk, or haven't you noticed?'

She said, 'I find our present surroundings quite congenial enough, Mr Grant, and I work office hours.'

'I see,' he said. 'You disappoint me, Ms Linton. I'd begun to think you were the real thing, for a change, but you're just another married lady playing at career woman. Pity,' he added with a shrug, and walked away.

She watched him go with sudden apprehension. She might be the blue-eyed girl where Barney was concerned, but if Rohan Grant relayed the gist of their conversation to him, then she would be in deep trouble.

Perhaps she even deserved to be. She seemed to have misconstrued his motives pretty thoroughly. But it was far better for him to write off her conduct as boorish, than to know the truth—that even the prospect of sharing a conventional *tête à tête* dinner with him frightened her half to death. She did not want to be alone with him, ever, or on any terms of intimacy. She wanted all future dealings with *Eve* to be with Mr

McDowell and Mr Handson. She wished Rohan Grant had stayed in Paris and rubber-stamped his approval of that campaign from a distance.

What's happening to me, she asked herself desperately, with a little shiver. She was beginning to feel positively light-headed. Perhaps in reality the radio alarm had never gone off that morning, and she was still in bed, having some nightmare.

Somebody from the accounts department came over to her. 'Barney says don't forget to let us have the bill for that dress,' he said in an undertone.

She said, 'I'd prefer to pay for it myself. That way, I can give it to a jumble sale with a clear conscience.'

He gasped at her. 'Cassie, are you mad? It looks terrific on you. I'd hardly have known you.'

'I hardly know myself,' Cass said hardily, 'And I don't like it. Back to reality tomorrow.' She made her way towards Barney. He was not, she noted with relief, talking to Rohan Grant, or anywhere near him. She touched his arm. 'Would it be all right if I went home now. I have a slight headache.'

He was all concern. 'I hope you're not coming down with the same damned thing as Roger.' He peered at her frowning. 'You're very pale,' he added accusingly. 'You'd better take a taxi. Charge it to expenses.'

Cass nodded wanly, and made her way to the cloakroom. Her clothes were there, in the boutique carrier, but she felt disinclined to change. It could wait till she got home, she decided.

And the headache hadn't been just an excuse. It turned into a real one on the journey, most of which Cass spent with her eyes closed.

'Good party?' the driver asked cheerfully as she paid him.

'The best,' she said.

Mrs Barrett's brows climbed almost into her hair when she answered her bell. 'My goodness,' she exclaimed. 'What a transformation.' Then she caught herself guiltily. 'Not that you don't always look nice, Mrs Linton.'

Cass smiled at her wearily. 'Is Jodie all right?' She shook her head. 'I'm sorry I couldn't make the open day, but . . .' she spread her hands helplessly.

'Well, she was naturally disappointed,' Mrs Barrett admitted. 'But I think she's over it now. I made some of that flapjack she likes for tea, and she's watching television. She'll be thrilled you're home early.'

'You look different,' was Jodie's instant greeting.

Cass kissed her. 'Different better, or different worse,' she asked teasingly.

'I don't know.' Jodie wriggled free. 'You didn't come,' she accused.

'Sweetheart, I couldn't.' Cass stroked her hair, grieving inwardly. She should have been with her daughter that afternoon, not dressed up like a Christmas tree, trying to make an impression on a man who combined too much money, and too much power, with infinitely too much sex appeal.

She shivered again. Well, at least now she'd admitted why he frightened her so. It was easy to armour oneself, when there was no temptation to break out of its protection, she thought sombrely.

After Brett, it had been easy to swear her private vow of total celibacy. Easy to keep it too. Now, in the course of one afternoon, everything had changed. Nothing was simple any more, and might never be so again, and if she didn't take some aspirin soon and lie down, her head would probably burst.

She listened to Jodie's excited account of the open day activities, sampled the flapjack, and accepted gratefully Mrs Barrett's carefully written account of everything Jodie's teacher had said about her brightness and promise. After the dark beginning to her child's life, it was the kind of thing she needed to hear.

She made herself a drink with fresh lemons, when she was in her own flat, and took the promised aspirin, but when she opened her eyes the next morning, everything was infinitely worse, and she closed them again groaning.

She ached everywhere fiercely, and would have burned up, if she hadn't felt so cold all the time. But she dragged herself out of bed, and made Jodie's breakfast.

When Mrs Barrett arrived to collect Jodie, she took one horrified look at Cass's grey face and shivering body, and ordered her back to bed.

'It's this forty-eight hour thing that's going round,' she said portentously. 'They say the doctors won't even come out for it—just tell you to keep warm, and drink plenty. I'll keep Jodie with me for a couple of days, while you sleep it off.'

Cass thanked her hoarsely, and tottered back to bed. After which life became a blur for several hours. She was vaguely conscious of Mrs Barrett bringing jugs of squash, and telling her she had 'phoned the agency to warn them she wouldn't be in. She tried to say something grateful in return, but it came out as a croak.

'Poor little soul,' Mrs Barrett said, perhaps then, or maybe much later. 'Not much more than a kid herself.'

Cass wondered why Mrs Barrett should be talking about her to her in that odd way, and fell almost at once into a profound and dreamless sleep.

Or thought she did. But the next time she opened her eyes, it seemed that Rohan Grant was there, sitting in the old armchair by the window, and she turned over, burying her flushed face in the pillow to dispel him, and muttering peevishly to herself.

Wasn't having 'flu bad enough? Did it have to be accompanied by more nightmares?

The next time she woke, he had gone, and she breathed a sigh of relief, stretching out aching limbs and muscles, and discovering wonderingly that she actually felt a little better, and might be persuaded to live, after all.

And when Mrs Barrett appeared, with a tray holding a cup of home-made vegetable soup, and a few wafer thin slices of brown bread and butter, Cass began to think that living might even be enjoyable again. She drank the soup to the last drop, while Mrs Barrett beamed at her.

'Slept the clock round, you have, dear,' she said. She looked slightly roguish. 'I don't think you even woke up for your visitor.'

Cass put down the bowl. 'Visitor?' she asked, trying to sound casual, but aware that her heart was hammering uncomfortably.

'From your work.' Mrs Barrett gave an unmistakable wink. 'Said they were worried about you, so I let him in for a while, although I kept popping in, just in case,' she added. 'I hope I did right, dear?'

Cass tried to assemble coherent thought. 'What was he like?' she enquired apprehensively.

Mrs Barrett's smile widened. 'Tall,' she said wistfully. 'A real dish.' She lowered her voice confidentially. 'And sexy with it. Made me wish I was thirty years younger, I can tell you.'

'How odd,' Cass said pallidly. 'He makes me wish I was thirty years older.'

Mrs Barrett didn't seem to hear her. 'I thought to myself—well that explains the pretty dress, and the way of doing your hair, and I was so pleased for you. Jodie liked him too,' she added.

'She met him?' Cass's head felt hollow.

'When I came up—to make sure everything was all right—she came with me, and they had a nice little chat.' Mrs Barrett gave her an anxious look. 'It *was* all right, wasn't it, Mrs Linton? When I looked in, he was sitting in that chair over there, and he said you'd been restless so he'd given you a drink, and made your pillows more comfortable. I'm sure no one could have been more concerned, that's why I thought . . .' her voice tailed off lamely.

Cass was burning again, but this time with embarrassment, not delirium. She managed a taut smile. 'No, he isn't a boyfriend,' she said quietly. 'Just—a colleague of sorts, and I can't imagine why he should have gone to all this trouble.'

'Flowers he brought too,' said Mrs Barrett. 'I left them in your living room, because my mother

used to say flowers in a sick room could be funny.
I'll get them for you, now you're awake.' She
bustled off to return a moment later with about a
ton of freesias arranged in an ornamental basket.
'Don't they smell lovely,' she said ecstatically.
'I'll put them on the chest of drawers where you
can see them.'

She was right about that, Cass thought wearily
later. Wherever she looked in the room, the
freesias seemed to be there, in the corner of her
eye. When she got up to go to the bathroom, she
carried them back into the living room, and put
them in the middle of the small dining table. She
didn't want them in her bedroom, reminding her
constantly of him—the interloper who'd been
there. Not a dream, not delirium, but reality.
And how dared he? she thought, trying to work
herself up into a rage, but finding she was still
too listless to make the effort. All she really
wanted to do was cry weakly, but she couldn't do
that. She'd shed her last tear a long time ago.

When evening came, she felt well enough to get
up. She ate the supper which Mrs Barrett
provided—a fluffy omelette flanked by grilled
tomatoes—by the fire, then switched on the
television. Some commercials which she and
Roger had designed for a client were scheduled
for their first showing, and Cass hadn't been
entirely happy about the filming. The client, a
fitted kitchen manufacturer, had insisted on
having a particular actress feature in the
commercials for reasons, Cass gathered, of a
sexual rather than an artistic nature. Roger had
roared with laughter about it, but Cass hadn't
been so amused, watching take after take being

ruined. And the girl was still wooden, she thought, viewing the finished product critically. If the fitted kitchen industry collapsed, she would probably never work again. Or if the client's wife found out, Cass thought drily.

As she switched off the set, she heard her front door buzzer. Mrs Barrett, she thought, returning for the tray.

'Come in,' she called. 'It isn't locked.'

She sank gratefully back on to the sofa, curling her legs under her.

He said, 'Don't you think you should keep it locked. I might have been a burglar.'

Cass jumped, every nerve ending jangling, as she stared at him, leaning against the door jamb.

She said, stammering, 'What—what are you doing here?'

'Checking the invalid's progress,' he said pleasantly, and strolled forward.

She said hurriedly, 'I'm fine,' aware as she spoke, that she was involuntarily tucking the folds of her dressing gown further around her feet and legs, and that the hazel eyes had taken sardonic note of her action.

'Yes, I'd like to sit down,' he said mockingly. 'And, no, I won't have any coffee, thank you.'

Cass flushed. 'Well, I'm not offering,' she said grittily. 'Perhaps you'd leave.'

'Not when I've only just got here.' He shrugged off the supple suede car coat he was wearing, and dropped it across the arm of the sofa, then sat down opposite her, stretching out long legs. He was more casually dressed this evening, she couldn't help noticing, with dark brown pants moulding themselves to his body,

and topped by a matching roll neck cashmere
sweater. She looked away hurriedly, fiddling with
the sash of her robe. 'Besides, I want to talk to
you, and you were in no fit state for conversation
when I called yesterday.'

'Why did you?' She glared at him.

'To see if your sudden illness was genuine, or
just a convenient excuse for avoiding me.'

'You flatter yourself, Mr Grant,' Cass said
defiantly. 'I'm hardly concerned enough about
you and your boundless male egotism to go to
those lengths.'

He raised eyebrows. 'You never miss a chance,
do you, Cass? I'll bet you're the pride of the local
sisterhood. Even when you're struggling back
from the 'flu, you're punching your weight.
Actually, I thought I should reassure you.'

'About what?' She gave him a wary look.

'The *Eve* cosmetics account.' He paused. 'You
seemed to think there might be—strings attached.
You're wrong.' He gave her a long look. 'And
you're also wrong if you thought I'd tell Finiston
about your unique method of turning down
dinner invitations.' His smile was thin. 'So if you
were expecting repercussions, there's no need.'

Cass bit her lip. She couldn't pretend that it
wasn't a relief. 'Thank you,' she acknowledged
stiltedly.

'Please don't mention it,' he said, too courteously. 'Now the next item on the agenda. Why
the hell did you hand me all that "I'm a married
woman" garbage, when you've been a widow for
at least four years?'

Cass lifted her head defiantly. 'To try and
convince you that I wasn't interested in you or your

invitations. You didn't seem prepared to take no for an answer.' She paused. 'How did you find out?'

'A few casual questions at Finiston Webber. It was amazing the amount of information that was volunteered.'

'Including my address,' she said bitterly.

He laughed. 'No, I got that from the telephone book. So, if you want to keep my visits here as another of your little secrets, then there's nothing to stop you.' He linked his hands behind his head, and watched her from beneath lazily drooping lids. 'Your colleagues regard you as something of an enigma, did you know that?'

'It's not something they're likely to discuss with me,' she said flatly. 'Perhaps you'd extend me the same courtesy, and keep out of my personal affairs.'

He gave her a mocking look. 'But there don't seem to have been any, Cass. Even the mildest approaches have had the brush-off. Why? And don't tell me your heart's in the grave,' he added cynically. 'The vibrant creature who sold me an advertising campaign didn't give that impression at all.'

'That's typical masculine arrogance,' she said stormily, her breasts rising and falling jerkily. 'None of you can believe that it's possible for a woman to lead a full, satisfying life without a—a tame stud somewhere in the background.' She took a deep breath. 'Well, believe this, Mr Grant. I've been married. My husband is dead. I have a child and a career, and I love both of them. There's no need, no room in my life for another—relationship. Incredible as it must seem, I'm just not interested.'

The long lashes lifted, and the brilliant hazel eyes searched her flushed passionate face remorselessly. 'Do you prefer women perhaps?'

The breath caught in her throat. 'Oh.' She almost threw herself off the sofa. 'Of course. The obvious explanation. If not one sexual connotation, then another. My God, you make me sick.' She paused, swallowing thickly. 'Now—get out. Just because I don't fancy you, doesn't give you the right to force yourself into my home and insult me.'

'Is that what I did?' He rose, and, barefoot as she was, she felt dwarfed although she'd always regarded herself as being of reasonable height for a woman. But it wasn't just a physical thing, she thought. It was a question of personality, an aura of vibrant, sensual masculinity which was almost tangible, making the small living room seem cramped.

He said softly, 'Why the hostility, Cass? Why the aggression? When other men have tried to get near you, you've always let them down lightly. What makes my treatment so different? From the moment you ran into my arms in that corridor, you looked as if you'd been poleaxed. All afternoon, I was watching those beautiful wounded eyes, and asking myself "Why?" I'm still wondering.'

'Because for a moment you reminded me of my late husband,' she said shortly. 'Now, will you please go?'

The dark brows snapped together, and his mouth compressed tautly. He gave a short, unamused laugh. 'I suppose I should have expected that. But I didn't.' He shook his head.

'All right, Cass, I'll go and leave you to convalesce in peace.'

At the front door, he paused, the lean tanned face sardonic. 'Well, good evening, Ms Linton. It's been—instructive, if nothing else. And I forgive you for lying to me about your marriage. Because, I have to confess, I lied to you too. I implied my dinner invitation had no sexual motive. It wasn't true. I wanted to get you into bed, Cass. I still want to, and I will.'

Before she could guess his intention or take evasive action, he took her by the shoulders, pulling her towards him in one swift, effortless movement. She cried out, but the sound was instantly muffled under the brief, searing pressure of his mouth.

It was over almost at once. He smiled at her.

'And sooner,' he said softly, 'rather than later. Sleep well, darling.'

And was gone.

CHAPTER THREE

CASS was still shaking two hours later, but from rage, she assured herself over and over again, not any other emotion.

She turned and punched savagely at an inoffensive sofa cushion. The sheer sexual arrogance of the creature. He clearly hadn't listened to one word she'd said, so securely armoured in his own conceit that it made him deaf to any point of view but his own.

And when she got back to work, gallingly, she would have to maintain a surface civility towards him at least. Or she could go to Barney, and ask to be taken off the account, she thought frowningly, only that would involve her in all kinds of explanations, she would much prefer to avoid.

But there had to be some way to convince the Rohan Grants of this world that she was not just—there for the taking, the frustrated widow of joke and insinuation.

She hated milky drinks, but she made one for herself before she went to bed, in the hope that it would help her sleep, then lay tossing and turning until far into the night.

But contrary to all expectations, she felt fine when she woke the next morning. Perhaps temper had helped burn out the few remaining germs, she thought drily.

After breakfast, she went downstairs to collect Jodie.

'I see your visitor was back,' Mrs Barrett commented archly as she let Cass in.

Cass smiled coolly. 'A little problem at work.' And that was putting it mildly, she added silently.

'Well, I don't know,' Mrs Barrett said, vexed. 'You'd think they'd leave you alone when you're poorly.'

'There's no justice, Mrs B.,' Cass said cheerfully. 'But I'll take care it doesn't happen again.' And how.

Her reunion with her daughter was everything she could have desired. Until they got back to their own flat, that is.

'Mrs Barrett's nice,' Jodie remarked. 'She lets me watch unsuitable things on television. She calls it "the box".'

Cass's lip quivered. 'How do you know they're unsuitable, madam?'

'Because you always change channels when they come on. You think I don't notice, but I do,' Jodie said serenely. 'Is that man coming back?'

Cass's heart skipped a beat. 'What—man?' She tried to sound casual.

'The one who came to see you. Mrs Barrett said he came again yesterday.' Jodie's face was angelic. 'Is he going to be my Daddy?'

'No, he is not,' Cass said forcibly.

Jodie gave a heavy sigh. 'I liked him.'

Cass gave her a long look. 'Jodie—you didn't say anything to him, did you?'

'What about?' Jodie didn't meet her gaze—a bad sign.

'About being your Daddy,' Cass said desperately.

The answer was too long in coming. 'No-o-o,' Jodie said, slowly and evasively.

'Jodie,' Cass threatened.

Her daughter's mouth trembled. 'He didn't mind, Mummy. He wasn't cross.' She ventured an appealing look. 'He laughed.'

'I bet he's never stopped,' Cass said savagely. 'What on earth possessed you?' She sighed, running a distracted irritable hand through her hair. 'Never—ever say such a thing to a visitor again.'

'Mrs Barrett said he was your boyfriend.'

'Well, Mrs Barrett was wrong,' Cass said with unwonted sharpness. She saw Jodie flinch, and gentled her tone. 'Sweetheart, he's a client—a very important man at my work. Not Daddy material at all,' she added, trying to make a belated joke of it all.

'He said he'd be honoured,' Jodie said mournfully.

Cass could have screamed.

She supposed reluctantly, thinking it over later, that it was to his credit that he'd been kind to the child—let her down lightly. But it didn't make her like him any better, or add relish to the prospect of having to face him again.

She was quite well enough to return to work on Monday morning. Roger was also back, delighted at the acquisition of the *Eve* account, but far more interested, Cass thought amusedly, in the lingering symptoms of 'flu which he was convinced still afflicted him.

And when he'd disposed regretfully of his various aches and pains, he then wanted to discuss Rohan Grant. Compared with whom, even Roger's health was a more acceptable topic, Cass thought crossly.

She steeled herself to answer his questions coolly and concisely trying not to give any of her personal feelings away.

'And you don't like him,' Roger said when she'd finished, proving that she was no actress.

'Do I have to?' Cass asked rather sourly. 'I wasn't too keen on Randy Sid, King of the Stainless Steel Sink either, but it made no difference to the campaign.'

'So you'd put the high-flying Mr Grant in the same category, would you?' Roger gave her a thoughtful glance. 'What happened Cass? Don't tell me he made a pass at you,' he added grinning.

'All right, I won't.' She made a business of searching in her desk drawer for something.

'You mean he did?' He sounded almost awed. 'Dear God.' He whistled. 'The guy's supposed to have an eye for women, but he must have laser vision if he could penetrate that battle dress top, and all the other ethnic layers you're usually cocooned in. How do you turn him on, Cassie? With the dance of the seven Greenham Common ponchos?'

'Very amusing.' Cass slammed the drawer, narrowly missing removing her own finger in the process. 'I had no idea that my love life, or lack of it, was of such consuming interest to everyone here.'

Roger said quietly, 'Actually, I was joking, but if I've offended you, Cass, then I'm truly sorry.' He paused. 'Has it happened at last? Has someone—some man really got to you?'

'No,' she said controlledly. 'Why do you ask?'

He shrugged. 'Because it has to happen sometime.' He frowned swiftly. 'Yet not, I'd have thought, with Rohan Grant.' He gave her a troubled look. 'He's the big league, Cass. His reputation says he likes to love them and leave them. Any relationship with him would be high on passion and good times, but lacking in anything else, including longevity.'

She smiled coolly. 'My sentiments entirely, so I'm in no danger.' She picked up some of the papers on her desk. 'This fireplace company. It seems to me the designs they want to feature in their ads are the really ugly ones. How can we explain that tactfully?'

She was passing Accounts on her way out to lunch later when a man came out. She recognised him as the one who'd spoken to her about the bill for her dress at the lunch party, and spontaneously they smiled at each other. He fell in beside her.

'Have you given it to the jumble sale yet?'

She laughed. 'I'm waiting for a good cause.' She was trying to remember his name. They'd been introduced when he joined Finiston Webber just before Christmas. Lloyd, she thought. That was it—Lloyd Haswell.

He said, 'Where do you go for lunch?'

She shook her head. 'I rarely do. I cook in the evenings for myself and my daughter, and I generally use my lunch hours for shopping.'

'Oh,' he said. 'I was going to ask you if you'd join me. There's a pub I go to that does a marvellous steak and kidney pie. Unless, of course, you're a vegetarian,' he added doubtfully.

'No,' Cass said cheerfully. 'I'm an unashamed carnivore still.' She stole a fleeting look at him under her lashes. He was about her own age or slightly older, nice looking, slightly diffident in his manner. Almost as different from Rohan Grant as it was possible to get. She added, 'Actually, I am quite hungry. I'm getting over 'flu, and I haven't felt like eating a great deal over the weekend.'

His face lit up. 'Does that mean I have company?'

'I'm afraid so,' she returned gaily, refusing to feel guilty at his obvious pleasure. If the consensus of opinion was that she needed a man in her life, then she would have one, she decided coldly and clinically. Someone nice and inoffensive like this Lloyd, whom she could keep at arm's length when it mattered. She wanted someone to be seen with; someone to convince Rohan Grant that he was wasting his time.

It might not be fair to Lloyd, she thought with compunction, but it wouldn't do him any lasting damage either.

In the event, she found him good company, with a ready sense of humour. When he mentioned a new West End comedy, and said he was thinking of getting tickets, it was no hardship at all to agree to go with him.

They arrived back at the agency together, and she guessed that the news would spread rapidly. At one time she would have found this painful, but there were worse threats hovering over her now than a little office gossip.

When she got to her own office, Roger was there, just replacing the telephone receiver.

He said 'McDowell's been on from *Eve*.' He paused. 'He wanted to know if we'd definitely signed Tracey Kent for the perfume commercial.'

'Why did he want to know that?' Cass frowned slightly. 'Both he and Handson thought she was perfect.'

Roger sighed. 'Orders from above,' he said laconically. 'Apparently the big boss wants Serena Vance to do the launch.'

'And does he know we haven't an icicle's chance in hell of getting Serena Vance?' Cass asked crisply.

Roger shrugged. 'He thinks we have. Apparently he and Miss Vance—know each other very well, and she will be happy to star in the *Eve* commercial as a favour to him.' He leered. 'Makes you wonder, doesn't it, just what he did for her?'

Cass said with distaste, 'I'd prefer not to.' She managed a little laugh. 'So—we're stuck with the Randy Sid syndrome all over again.'

'Well, hardly,' Roger objected. 'At least Serena Vance can act. But we'll have to re-jig her script. The words that would have been acceptable from someone who looked as dewily innocent as Tracey would be ludicrous spoken by Miss Vance.'

Cass fiddled with her pen. 'Of course, we don't really know if she'll do it,' she pointed out. 'Perhaps Rohan Grant is just—shooting a line.'

'Perhaps, but I don't think so,' Roger said drily. 'What would be the point? No, I bet when shooting starts, the camera will be lingering over Miss Vance's deservedly famous attributes, instead of Tracey's innocent charms.' He sighed enviously. 'What a thing it is to have power, as well as good looks and charisma. I wish Serena Vance owed me a favour,' he added disconsolately.

When she got home that night, Cass went through a pile of old colour supplements which she had put out for collection by the dustmen, until she found the one, dated a few months earlier, which she wanted. Serena Vance's challenging beauty stared up from the cover beneath the legend—'Serena Vance—sex symbol or serious actress?' Cass couldn't remember what, if any, conclusion the article inside had come to, but she did recall the other full page photograph which had accompanied it, showing the actress naked except for a few discreetly placed folds of an opulent wild mink cloak. A present, the caption had stated, from an admirer.

'I wonder who that was!' Cass muttered to herself, thrusting the magazine back into the pile.

It had come, she told herself, as no great surprise to learn that Rohan Grant had been the lover of someone like the voluptuous Serena. Nevertheless it made his subsequent behaviour towards herself all the more baffling and ridiculous. Unless, of course, he was just amusing himself at her expense—tormenting her to see how she would react. A young widow with a reputation as a loner would seem easy game for a man used to finding his pleasures with sophisticated beauties.

It was a train of thought which should have made her angry, but instead she found herself getting more and more depressed, although she reminded herself that was probably the aftermath of the 'flu.

She cooked supper, had a game of draughts with Jodie before putting her to bed, then settled down with notepad and pen to watch some television. There were several important contracts coming up for renewal at the agency, and she wanted to do a critical breakdown on some of the commercials already running, to show how the campaigns could be improved and up-dated.

But it was difficult, she found, keeping her mind on her work for once. It kept straying, almost obsessively, back to her various encounters with Rohan Grant, analysing them, trying to discover why she'd reacted to him as she had. Remembering particularly that last confrontation when he had told her openly that he intended to seduce her. Remembering his touch—that brief kiss with painful, disturbing clarity.

She thrust the pad and pen away from her with hands that shook. Fool, she castigated herself. He didn't mean it—any of it. He was just having a little game at your expense, because you annoyed him by turning him down. He decided he'd give you something to think about, and by sitting brooding like this over his nonsense, you're playing right into his hands.

She looked round the living room and sighed. The flat wasn't large, but it was enough for her needs and Jodie's and she'd become casually fond of the place. Now, the walls seemed to be closing in on her, making her feel trapped—restless.

She bit her lip. Maybe she should take Mrs Barrett up on her eager offers to babysit. She had the theatre next week to look forward to, but there were other things too. The cinema, for one instance, and Roger and his wife for another.

They were always inviting her for meals, and she'd usually refused, terrified that they might try to matchmake by inviting some spare man of their acquaintance. And yet what had she to fear from such casual meetings?

Staying in alone was no safeguard, and nor was wearing deliberately dowdy clothes. Her real security was Brett's memory, and the knowledge that, after him, there could never be another man for her.

The past. Her secret armour against the world—and against a man like Rohan Grant in particular.

She bought a new dress for the theatre trip, a silky turquoise thing with a loosely bloused top. Oh, Barney, what did you start, she thought, as she stared back at the attractive stranger she saw in the fitting room mirror.

It got Jodie's unqualified approval too.

'You look like a fairy princess,' she said ecstatically. 'Are you going with that man?'

Cass smiled at her. 'I'm going with a man, darling, but not that one. A very nice man, too,' she added as Jodie's face visibly drooped.

Lloyd was proving to be extremely pleasant company. He didn't try to monopolise her at work, but they'd had lunch a couple of times together. She'd almost invited him to call for her at the flat, instead of meeting in the foyer, but decided to stick to the prior arrangement. It wouldn't be fair, she thought, to arouse hopes in Lloyd which she had no intention of fulfilling.

But the admiration in his eyes when they met was warming, and so was the thoughtfulness which had instigated the box of chocolates he handed her.

'I thought this had gone out of fashion since people started counting calories,' she laughed.

'You don't need to count anything,' he told her seriously. 'If anything, you could do with a little more weight. You look quite frail sometimes.'

Cass felt a giggle rising, and hastily suppressed it. Was that the image he had of her? The brave little widow, battling against the odds of a hostile world? She wondered if he would be too disillusioned if she told him she was as tough as old boots, then the crowds at the theatre entrance parted like the Red Sea, and all desire to laugh left her.

Lloyd nudged her. 'My God,' he sounded awe-struck. 'That's Serena Vance, the film star. And do you see who she's with?'

'Yes,' Cass said. 'I do. Let's find our seats, Lloyd. Just because everyone else is staring at them doesn't mean we have to join in.'

He gave her a surprised look. 'Aren't you interested?'

'I shall have plenty of opportunity to study Miss Vance in depth next month,' Cass said drily. 'Didn't you know? She's doing the commercials for the *Eve* perfumes. Barney signed her two days ago.'

Lloyd sighed. 'I knew the accounts department was the wrong one to belong to,' he said mournfully. 'Can you wangle me an introduction?'

Cass laughed rather forcedly. 'You could probably take Roger's place. He met her with Barney, and came back moaning that he couldn't get anywhere near her because the scent she's currently using brings on his asthma.'

'Well it obviously doesn't have the same effect on Mr Grant,' Lloyd said with a chuckle. 'Judging by the way she was clinging to his arm, she looked as if she'd been welded to him.'

'What a boost to his ego that must be,' Cass muttered. 'As if he needed one.'

Their seats were in the circle, and it took all her self-control not to lean forward and scan the stalls below.

The play was as light as a bubble—a risque comedy about the efforts of a practised womaniser to seduce the beautiful divorcee who'd moved into the flat opposite his, and everyone except Cass seemed to think it riotous. I must be losing my sense of humour, she thought ruefully, as she joined in obediently with everyone else's amusement. Her sympathies were with the divorcee every step of the way.

In the interval she allowed herself to be reluctantly persuaded to go for a drink. She stood in the shelter of a potted palm, and waited while Lloyd fought his way to the bar, her eyes sifting the crowd nervously. Her reactions, she thought, were totally unreasonable, but knowing that didn't alter them by one iota.

And when Rohan's voice from behind her said coolly, 'Good evening,' she nearly jumped out of her skin.

She said, 'Oh, hello' and looked wildly round for Lloyd's return.

He said, 'Serena, this is Ms Linton the genius who is going to put *Eve* back on the map.'

Serena Vance offered a token handshake, light

and dismissive. She said plaintively, 'Darling, the curtain will be going up on the second act at any moment, and I'm dying for a drink. You ordered them didn't you? Do we have to stay huddled in this corner?'

'Of course not,' Rohan turned to Cass. 'May I get you something?'

'No thank you.' She could see Lloyd struggling through the crowd with their drinks. 'My escort is just coming.'

Serena Vance gave him the quick all encompassing glance Cass guessed she would give any man, and mentally wrote him off. It was charmingly done, with a smile and a handshake that lasted a great deal longer than the previous one, but Cass wasn't fooled. The fabulous Serena might light up like an electric bulb for any man, but visits to the power station would be strictly allocated according to money and power, she decided cynically.

'Haswell?' Rohan was saying. 'You work at Finiston Webber too do you?'

'In the Accounts department,' Lloyd confirmed, looking in a dazed way as if Christmas and his birthday had suddenly occurred on the same day.

'How fascinating,' Serena drawled. 'And will you be personally involved in this commercial I'm making?'

'Alas no.' Lloyd shook his head. 'It's Cassie here who's the ideas girl.'

'Really?' Serena Vance gave Cass another, longer look. It seemed to Cass to be warning her not to get any ideas beyond those needed for the commercial, but she decided that was probably her imagination working overtime.

People were beginning to stare at them, she noticed with embarrassment, nudging each other as they recognised Serena, peering at her companions and trying to place them in the same glamorous milieu.

Rohan said easily, 'I'll get those drinks.'

Serena watched him go, the full curves of her lovely painted mouth taking on a sudden hard line. It was clear she would have preferred to go with him.

Cass toyed with the idea of saying brightly, 'I'm sorry we're such dull company,' but decided against it. After all, she was going to have to work with the woman, and she'd already heard along the grapevine that Serena's temperament when she was filming in no way matched her name.

Lloyd said eagerly, 'There's a vacant table just behind us. Would you like to sit down, Miss Vance.'

Miss Vance gave it a quick look, deciding immediately that it would put her at a disadvantage by removing her from the centre of attention. 'I'd prefer to stand,' she declared sweetly. 'Theatre seats seem so cramped these days.'

A woman came up at that moment and asked her to sign her programme, and Serena complied graciously, murmuring that it was so long since she'd been in dear, beautiful London, that she really hadn't expected to be recognised.

Cass sipped her white wine, and reflected that appearing on breakfast television on both channels was hardly the way to guarantee anonymity.

When Rohan returned, Serena was almost surrounded by autograph hunters and well-wishers, and obviously loving every minute of it, her face more animated than Cass had seen it.

'Enjoying the play?' Cass looked up to find Rohan beside her, Lloyd having joined the crowd of excited fans around Serena.

'Not particularly,' she said coldly. 'It's not a subject I find very appealing.'

'Trying to make me believe you're a prude, Cassie?' The hazel eyes glinted down at her. 'You won't succeed. Your mouth—the lower lip in particular—tells a very different story.'

She stared down impotently into her glass, feeling a helpless tide of colour rising in her face.

'The pursuit of the human female by the male may not fit in with your own philosophy,' he went on. 'But without it the species would have died out a long time ago.'

'In some cases, I can see where that would have been an advantage,' Cass said bitingly. 'Now will you please leave me alone?'

'I don't know whether that's possible,' Rohan said almost reflectively. The hazel eyes looked coolly, disturbingly into hers. '"While I am I and you are you"' he quoted softly. '"So long as the world contains us both ..."' He paused. 'I'm sure I don't need to go on.'

'You had no need to begin.' Cass put down her glass, her hands shaking. 'And can I point out that you are not Robert Browning, and in no way am I Elizabeth Barrett.'

He laughed. 'I think, on the whole, she may have given him the easier time.'

Cass shrugged, listening avidly for the bell which would signal the commencement of the second act. Would it never ring? she wondered miserably. 'If it's an easy time you want,' she said, 'I suggest you transfer your attentions to your companion. I'm sure you'd find her more than receptive.'

His brows lifted. 'Showing your claws, Cass?' he asked with dry appreciation. 'A disinterested bystander listening to you might wonder if you could possibly be jealous.'

'Then he would not only be disinterested, but misinformed,' she said sharply, hearing with a rush of relief the sound of the bell above the hum of laughter and chat around them. 'I don't care what women you favour, Mr Grant, as long as I'm not one of them. I just want to be left in peace.'

'Those bruised eyes I saw when we first met don't indicate a particularly peaceful existence, Cass. What are you frightened of?'

'I'm not frightened at all,' she denied hurriedly, aware that the group round Serena Vance was breaking up reluctantly, that the actress was rising and Lloyd was coming towards them. 'Just—bored, and rather irritated with all this hassle. I don't need it.'

Rohan shrugged, his gaze taking one last relentless look. 'Very well,' he said. 'Then I'll do as you wish. I'll—er transfer my attentions to where they'll be appreciated from now on. Does that reassure you?'

She didn't answer. She moved to Lloyd's side, slipping a hand through his arm with a deliberately possessive gesture. 'Ready?' she asked smilingly.

As they moved back to their seats, Lloyd shook his head, expelling his breath in a silent whistle.

'What an evening,' he muttered incredulously. 'What an evening.'

And for very different reasons, Cass could only agree.

CHAPTER FOUR

CASS got up the next morning, ruefully aware that she hadn't slept very well, and glad, under the circumstances, that it was the weekend which faced her, and not the office.

It was a sunny morning—Spring taking a firm hold on London at last, perhaps, after the cool showery weather of the past few weeks, and Cass, looking restlessly round the flat as she and Jodie ate breakfast, and Jodie investigated the remains of her box of chocolates, decided it was a good a time as any to remove the outward signs of a year's wear and tear.

'I think I'll get some paint and start on these walls,' she said. 'What colour shall I get?'

'Yellow,' said Jodie, as she always did. 'Like the sun,' she added unexpectedly, and Cass who'd been about to propose mushroom or caramel, paused, arrested.

Perhaps Jodie was right, she thought wrily. Maybe they needed some sunshine in their lives, even of the artificial variety.

'All right,' she agreed. 'We'll go and get it after breakfast.'

This accomplished, she began to transfer the movables, and as much of the furniture as she could manage, out of the living room, and cover up the rest, Jodie helping, although basically more interested in a picture she'd started of how the room would look when it was finished. An interior designer in the making, Cass wondered with a smile as she cleared bookshelves.

They ate a quick lunch of soup and scrambled eggs, then Cass began to wash down the existing paintwork. She considered herself competent at housework without being in love with it, and it was always shaming to discover how much accumulated grime lurked in little seen corners and along ledges.

She was rubbing vigorously at a length of skirting board when the front door buzzer sounded. She paused, puzzled, tempted not to answer it. It might be Lloyd, she thought with vague annoyance. He'd wanted to see her this weekend, and she'd made the excuse of prior commitments. He'd accepted this, albeit reluctantly, or she thought that he had, but all the same he might have decided against taking 'no' for an answer, which would be a problem.

She got up from her knees, stripping off her rubber gloves, and looking wrily down at her grey dungarees. They were old and baggy, and together with the scarf she'd wrapped round her head, were hardly the outfit she'd have chosen in which to receive callers.

She opened the door, her lips curving into a reluctant smile, already forming words of excuse which died on her lips when she saw Rohan confronting her.

'You?' Her voice was bitter. 'Your guarantees don't last long, Mr Grant. I hope Barney's had his lawyers go over our contract with you.'

His brows rose. 'I'm not breaking any agreements, Ms Linton.' His drawl emphasised with mockery the last two words. 'It isn't you that I've come to see,' he added, strolling past her, as Jodie with a squeal of pleasure ran to meet him. 'Hello, sweetheart.' He didn't stoop, he went down on his haunches in front of her. 'I've got my young nephews in the car outside. We're going to the zoo, and I thought you might like to come with us—if your mother permits, of course,' he added, his eyes meeting Cass's with cool irony.

'Oh, Mummy, may I?' Jodie's pleading gaze was fixed on her, and Cass suppressed an inner groan.

'But you'd need to change,' she began. 'And Mr Grant is obviously in a hurry.'

'Not in the slightest,' he corrected levelly. 'Take as long as you need, my pet.'

Jodie whooped with delight, and fled to her room, leaving them facing each other.

Cass said angrily, 'How dare you? Do you realise you made it impossible for me to refuse to let her go with you?'

'I do,' he said. 'It was quite deliberate, Cass. Why should your daughter be deprived of an afternoon's fun with kids of her own age, just because you don't like their uncle? And even if you're anti-zoo,' he added. 'At least you must admit that it will be more interesting for her than cooped up here with you, watching paint dry.'

'I'm quite capable of taking my child to the zoo myself,' she said sharply. 'She doesn't go short of pleasure trips.'

'But she goes short on male companionship,' he said curtly. 'That may be a deliberate ploy on your part, Cass, but I don't believe it's a healthy one, and I intend to redress the balance a little. Today is only the beginning.'

She gaspẹd furiously. 'You said you'd leave me alone.'

'I said I'd transfer my attentions where they'd be appreciated,' he returned. 'I think Jodie appreciates them, don't you?' He paused. 'Words are your *metier*,' he went on with soft mockery. 'Didn't your trained ear tell you I was being— slightly ambiguous in what I said?'

'No,' she snapped. 'Obviously I underestimated you, Mr Grant, yet again.'

Jodie came dancing back, changed with the speed of light into her new corded trousers with their matching waistcoat.

'I've put on my best clothes,' she announced.

'You look fantastic,' Rohan said.

'But you'll need a coat,' Cass warned, and Jodie's lip bulged ominously.

'But it's *sunny* today,' she began to protest, but Rohan intervened swiftly.

'It's cold just the same, darling. Simon and James have had to wear their anoraks.' He paused. 'You see, if you catch cold, your mother will never let you come out with me again, and I have all kinds of plans.'

Jodie's face cleared magically at this hint of future delights, and she vanished again.

'Bribery too,' Cass said disgustedly.

His brows lifted sardonically. 'You'd have preferred a scene?' he asked sardonically. 'Well— that figures.'

'I don't want Jodie to think these outings are going to be a regular occurrence,' she said. 'And we don't need your—amateur psychology either. If I feel Jodie is—lacking men's company, then I'll do something about it. I don't need your interference.'

'Don't tempt me to tell you what you do need.'
His voice was soft, but the glance which raked
down her body, stripping off the unbecoming
clothes, was an insult, and the colour stormed
into her face.

Jodie returned, forcing her arms into the
sleeves of her anorak. 'I did a picture,' she
announced. 'A picture of this room, all yellow
and pretty.' She fetched it from the table. 'That's
Mummy, in her blue dress she wore last night,
and that's you,' she added with satisfaction. 'You
can keep it if you like,' she went on magnani-
mously. 'I'll do another for Mummy.'

Rohan put down a hand and stroked back her
hair. 'I'll treasure it,' he said seriously. He folded
the paper, and put it in his wallet while Jodie
beamed.

Cass bit her lip. The original version, she
thought bitterly, had contained only Jodie and
herself. She'd had no idea that Jodie had made
any later additions, and she felt suffocated with
angry embarrassment.

'Goodbye, darling.' She smiled at Jodie,
ignoring Rohan's ironic gaze. 'Have—have a
lovely time, and please don't be late back.'

'I'll keep her safe,' Rohan said quietly. 'I'll
have the boys' mother to contend with as well as
you, if anything goes wrong,' he added drily.
'And I think my sister Marcia frightens me
marginally more than you do.' He paused. 'See
you later, Cass.'

The front door closed, and she was alone. She
went back to cleaning down the paintwork, but
the zest, if there'd been any, had gone out of it.

She'd been out-manoeuvred, she realised

angrily. But if Rohan Grant thought that he could reach her through Jodie, he was mistaken. And if he believed that Jodie's talk of Daddies and inclusion of him in her drawing meant anything either, then he was wrong about that too. In fact, his intervention in their lives could be little short of disastrous, she thought worriedly.

She wished that she'd responded more positively to Lloyd's plans. They could have gone to the coast, all three of them, so that Rohan Grant would have found the flat deserted when he called. She wrung out her cloth with a sigh. Lloyd was no less a man that Rohan Grant, but he was, in some unfair way, so much less of a threat.

He'd kissed her the previous night, gently, experimentally, and she'd found his advances pleasantly undemanding. No, it hadn't been the memory of Lloyd's lips which had robbed her of sleep, she thought savagely, but the total, if unwanted, recall of Rohan's brief, incisive possession of her mouth. The kiss had lasted seconds at most, yet it had left a remembrance like a scar in its wake. It should have been easy to put it out of her mind, and the fact that it wasn't easy at all, disturbed her.

But then, she realised, kneeling back on her heels, with a sudden shiver of apprehension, everything about Rohan Grant disturbed her.

She worked steadily through the afternoon, then took a swift bath, and washed her hair. She dried her hair grimly, subduing its soft waves into the former severity, and dressed herself in what she knew to be one of her least becoming dresses, a donkey brown tent which swamped her, and muddied the clear tones of her skin, adding ribbed tights, in spite of the weather's mildness, and flat shoes.

It was past six when they returned, and she opened the door, giving Rohan a coolly civil smile, instantly aware of the incredulity in his eyes as he took in her appearance.

'You haven't finished the room yet,' Jodie exclaimed disappointedly.

'Hold your horses.' Rohan followed her in, although that was not what Cass had intended. 'Your mother isn't Superwoman. And she's had some transformation work to do on herself as well as the decor,' he added softly.

'Did you have a good time?' Cass asked Jodie directly, ignoring him.

'It was wonderful,' Jodie said rapturously. She looked wonderful too, her cheeks full of colour, her eyes sparkling, and the marks of illicit lollies round her mouth. 'I liked the monkeys best. They did rude things, and James said . . .'

'I think we'll draw a veil over what James said,' Rohan interrupted her with amusement. 'Can't you tell your mother about something reasonably polite and educational—like the aviary, or watching the lions being fed?'

'Oh, I saw them too,' Jodie agreed. 'But the monkeys were *funny*.'

Cass nerved herself to speak to him. 'Thank you for giving her such a good time, and bringing her back so promptly,' she said, too politely. 'I hope you didn't find three children too much of a handful.'

'Jodie behaved impeccably,' he returned courteously. 'And Marcia wouldn't allow any child of hers to be a handful. I thoroughly enjoyed myself.'

'I'm starving,' Jodie brought in plaintively, and Rohan gave her hair a tweak.

'You've had tea, you appalling brat.'

'That was ages ago,' Jodie said wistfully. 'Are we going to have supper soon, Mummy, and can Rohan stay?'

Cass was aghast, on a number of counts. She said immediately, 'Jodie—you don't address Mr Grant by his first name. It isn't—respectful.'

'But he likes it,' Jodie said wide-eyed. 'And that's what James and Simon call him too.'

'I really do prefer it,' Rohan put in drily. 'I'm sorry if it upsets your susceptibilities, Cass. I didn't realise you were so conventional.'

Her lips tightened. She looked at Jodie again. 'Well, let that pass. But don't you think Mr Grant has been kind enough for one day? He's a very busy person, much in demand. He has other things to do this evening.'

'No,' he said silkily. 'Not a thing. I'd love to stay to supper.' He smiled at her across Jodie's head, his eyes meeting hers with the insolent message; *and breakfast too*.

In the voluminous folds of her skirt, Cass's nails curled into the palms of her hands.

'I'm sorry to seem inhospitable,' she said. 'But we're having goulash, and I'm afraid it's a small one, certainly not large enough for three,' she added with quiet satisfaction.

Jodie's face drooped instantly, but Rohan said easily, 'Then why don't we have something else.

The goulash will keep, I'm sure. Marcia always says casseroles taste better on the second day. I noticed a Kentucky fried chicken place just round the corner. Why don't we shock our well-ordered digestions with some junk food?'

Jodie crowed with pleasure, shooting her mother a triumphant look. Cass stood blankly, aware that once again the wind had been taken out of her sails, and wondering what she could do about it.

She started again, 'Jodie—it really isn't a good idea. The room's in a mess, smelling of paint, covered in dust sheets. Mr Grant won't want to stay.'

'He does, he said he did.' Jodie's face was full of reproach. 'I want him to stay.'

'Then there's nothing more to be said,' Rohan smiled down at her. 'Clear off the table, brat, and find some plates, and I'll be back presently.' As Jodie flew to obey, he said in an undertone, 'Don't spoil her day, Cass. She neither shares nor understands your hostility.'

'She hasn't the same reason,' Cass returned bitterly. 'You win again, it seems. Enjoy your little victories, Mr Grant. You're going to find them short-lived.'

He smiled. 'But I don't want war between us, Cass. I want peace—on my terms,' he added softly.

Cass cleared off the table and helped Jodie lay it. Jodie was bubbling, and although Cass knew that sooner or later she would have to have a serious talk with her, convince her somehow that Rohan Grant was not the right person to have in their lives, she knew that now was not the time.

When Rohan returned, he was carrying not just a carrier bag of food, but a bottle of wine from the local off-licence and coca cola for Jodie.

'It's like a feast,' Jodie said rapturously. 'I wish James and Simon had come too.'

'Next time, maybe,' he said, and Cass tensed in rejection of the casual words. There would be no next time.

'What did you do with your nephews,' she asked, trying to sound nonchalant. 'Leave them for the lions?'

He shook his head. 'Marcia's taking them down to the country tonight. Her husband's in oil out in the Gulf, and they've been with him there, but he's decided to send them home as the situation's currently not very stable. The boys will be starting school here after Easter, and Marcia will be staying at our family home for the time being. She's supposed to be looking for a house,' he added with a wry smile. 'But I'll bet she gives Bill more grey hairs by rushing back to join him as soon as the boys are settled.'

Cass put the food on to warmed plates. She didn't like the note of amused affection that he used when he spoke of his family. It made him seem too human. She needed to think of him as the high-powered tycoon who was steering a multi-national company pretty well unscathed through a world recession. Although what such a person had to do with the casually dressed, attractive stranger who was sitting at her small dining table, teasing Jodie as he poured coke into her glass, and preparing to eat chicken and chips, she hadn't the slightest idea.

The Rohan Grants of this world were more

usually found sealing million pound deals at Le Gavroche.

She ate her chicken, and drank her wine, dry and delicious, and listened indulgently to Jodie's excited chatter, conscious all the time that she was watching him more and more under her lashes. That all kinds of questions about him were surfacing in her mind, and not receiving satisfactory answers.

One thing was certain, she thought. Apart from that fleeting physical resemblance, evinced by their colouring, he was in no way like Brett. Her husband had never been so masterful, so totally sure of himself, the world, and his place in it. Perhaps if he had, then his life might have been very different, she thought with a little inward sigh. And, of course, she would not have married him at all. She didn't like men who dominated and manipulated, or who saw women in terms of bed only.

And that, she must never forget, was why Rohan Grant was here, eating a meal he would never have considered in ordinary circumstances, and charming her daughter. Because to him, it was all a means to an end. She'd injured his vanity by refusing to go out with him, and only her total capitulation to him sexually would salve the wound.

He has to prove he's so bloody irresistible, she told herself savagely, feeding her resentment, banishing the traitorous thought that the girl she'd once been might well have found Rohan Grant irresistible.

But not now. So why couldn't he be content with the Serena Vances of this world, and stop tormenting her? Perhaps the clue was in the poem he's mockingly quoted at her the previous night. She'd found her copy of Browning when she was shifting her books, and she'd looked it up, despising herself as she did so. '"Me the loving,"' she thought ironically. "And you the loth, While the one eludes, must the other pursue . . ."' Only there was no love involved, just the instincts of the hunter, intent on bringing down his prey.

The meal took much longer than she'd hoped, because Jodie discovered the fresh fruit salad she'd made, and it had to be served. She offered coffee with overt reluctance, hoping he would take the hint and leave, but he accepted with a sardonic lift of the eyebrow.

When she got back from the kitchen, she found with dismay that Jodie had produced a jigsaw, and that she and Rohan were already apparently absorbed in fitting together its frame.

She said hurriedly, 'It's too late to start that now, Jodie. It's nearly bedtime.'

'Oh, just a few minutes,' Jodie appealed. 'While Rohan has coffee,' she added beguilingly. 'And then he's going to tell me a story.'

'No, he isn't, sinner.' Rohan shook his head. 'Although he might tuck you in, if you don't make any more fuss about going to bed.'

Cass bit her lip. Those few quiet moments at the end of the day with Jodie were some of her most precious, and private. She enjoyed being with her daughter, chatting softly, soothing her into sleep with quiet laughter, banishing as far as she could night's shadows. The thought of this man, this stranger intruding into their time together was almost unbearable.

It was physically painful to her to see him with the child, winning her affection for selfish, degrading motives. She decided she would rather not watch, and went back into the kitchen, running water into the sink with angry energy.

She didn't realise she was no longer alone, until, having rinsed the last dish, she turned away to dry her hands and saw, with a start, that he was leaning in the doorway watching her, his hazel eyes inscrutable.

He said quietly, 'I notice you didn't join us.'

'I wanted to do the dishes,' she said shortly. 'And it's a very small bedroom. There's hardly room for more than one person beside Jodie.'

'That of course depends on the amount of space you require,' he said drily. 'I can see why you'd find the situation cramped.'

'Then I'd be glad if you'd carry your understanding a stage further and leave,' Cass said, hearing with panic the ragged note in her voice.

His brows lifted. 'I've met more gracious hostesses,' he said sardonically. 'Why such haste, Cass? Expecting the boyfriend?'

'No,' she denied unthinkingly, and could have bitten her tongue out.

'Then why?' he said. 'If you're as indifferent to me as you say, what the hell difference does it make whether I go or stay? What possible danger are you in?'

'None,' she said shrilly. 'I—I just prefer my own company.'

'Then you must have had an enjoyable afternoon,' he said pleasantly. 'You can't expect

to have your own way all the time, Cass. Life
isn't like that. Besides I'm not sure in your case
that too much solitude is good for you.' He
smiled at her, and she felt the unwilling pull of
his attraction, of that almost charismatic sexuality
which disturbed her so. 'And I know it isn't
good for me.'

'On the contrary,' Cass said between her teeth.
'I think a period spent as a hermit might be
extremely salutory for you.'

He laughed out loud. 'Do they allow double
beds into hermitages, Cass? I wouldn't go on
any other terms. Being cut off from the world
might have some attraction if you were with
me.'

'Please.' Her voice shook. 'Please—don't say
such things. You must know I hate them . . .'

'I know,' he said. 'And I wonder why.' He
paused and his voice gentled. 'Don't fight all the
time, Cassie. Relax a little. Come and sit with
me—finish the wine—watch some television, if
that's what you want. You look tired, and
stopping three lively kids from throwing themselves to the bears isn't my idea of a quiet
time either, although I wouldn't have missed it.'
He reached out a hand. 'Sit with me, Cass.
Please.'

Inexplicably she was moving towards him. Felt
her hand taken gently, herself led back into the
living room, where the sofa unshrouded from its
dust sheet waited in front of the glowing welcome
of the fire. She sank down on to its cushions,
looking almost with bewilderment at the wine
glass he put into her hand. A faint alarm bell
sounded in her head.

'I don't want any more to drink,' she began, and he put a silencing finger on her lips.

'You're fighting again, and tonight we've declared a truce,' he said softly. 'And I'm not filling you full of booze so that I can seduce you. It's not my style. I don't want our first time together blurred by alcohol, or anything else.'

She tried to summon the energy to tell him there would never be a first time for them, but all that emerged from her lips was a little sigh. She sipped her wine, and watched the steady flames of the gas fire, and felt almost imperceptibly, the tension seeping out of her.

She stole a sideways look at him, sitting at the other end of the sofa, very casual, very relaxed, the leather jerkin he'd been wearing discarded now, the sleeves of his shirt unbuttoned, and the cuffs turned back over tanned forearms. The neck of his shirt was undone too, revealing a brown muscular chest, faintly shadowed with hair.

Only the wealthy could afford a year-round tan, Cass thought idly, and, guiltily, caught herself wondering whether it extended to the whole of his body. There was no future in that kind of speculation, she thought, and was thankful he could have no idea what she'd been thinking.

Then she realised he was watching her too, and suddenly the long silence between them was loaded, but, in some strange way, with anticipation, not alarm.

He leaned towards her, taking the glass from her hand, and setting it down, before he drew her into his arms, so that she lay across him, cradled on his thighs. Then he began to kiss her, brushing her mouth with his in endless tiny caresses, that aroused but did not satisfy. His fingers slid through her hair touching her sensitive scalp with little stroking movements, then finding the vulnerable nape of her neck, and cupping it softly in the warmth of his hand as his mouth lingered on hers, letting the kiss deepen sweetly and enticingly. He was tormenting her again, she recognised dimly, tantalising her into opening her mouth, and offering him of her own free will the deeper intimacy he sought.

His other hand was at her waist, tracing its slenderness through the thick enveloping material of the brown dress, moving slowly and unhurriedly across the lower reaches of her rib cage, then down across the smooth flatness of her abdomen, and back to her waist. A gently exploring ellipse of a movement which never reached the surge of her small breasts, their nipples tautening in impatient desire against the constricting lace cups of her bra, or the sudden fierce tremulousness of her thighs.

Oh God, she'd never wanted anything in her life as much as she wanted his hands on her in desire. And he knew it. And that was why he was keeping her waiting this age, this lifetime, this eternity.

He was waiting for her surrender, and she gave it suddenly, urgently, her hands clinging to his shoulders, her mouth parting in swift intense demand. His response was immediate, and fiercely, passionately sensual, locking their mouths together in an erotic fusion totally outside any of her previous experience.

And at the same moment, his hands found her breasts, cupping them tenderly, intimately, as if the cumbersome folds of material between his warmth and hers did not exist.

As soon, she realised, they would not. One hand was already at her throat, releasing the first of the tiny buttons which fastened her dress from neck to waist.

She heard a moan rising in her throat, a moan of greed, of the necessity his kisses had forced into being.

But what echoed in her head was a scream, and then another. And another . . .

Rohan's hands had stilled. He lifted his mouth from hers, the hazel eyes staring down into hers in horrified enquiry.

She twisted off his lap, and ran to the bedroom where Jodie lay, her small body twisting restlessly, eyes tightly closed, as her mouth continued to utter those unearthly cries.

'Cass, what is it?' Rohan demanded tensely. He was beside her already bending towards Jodie, and she pulled at him frantically.

'No, don't touch her. She's having a nightmare. I know what to do. I can cope. Go—please.'

He went without protest, and Cass got on to the narrow bed, gathering her daughter in her arms, murmuring to her, stroking her hair, calling her the names of babyhood, until Jodie opened her eyes, shuddering, and said, 'Mummy?'

'I'm here, darling.'

'I thought—that man.' The small voice was woeful and terrified and Cass's heart contracted in pity.

'No, darling. There's no man. Everything's all right. It was just a nasty dream.'

'Just a dream,' Jodie repeated obediently. Within minutes she was asleep again, breathing softly and regularly.

Cass got up slowly and gingerly, fearful of disturbing her. In the early days, she'd stayed with Jodie all night sometimes, terrified of a recurrence, but gradually she'd realised that the nightmares, when they came, came singly.

Slowly, reluctantly, she went back to the living room, hoping against hope that Rohan might have taken her at her word and left altogether.

But he was there, waiting for her. He swung round impatiently as she entered.

He said without preamble, 'What brought that on?'

Cass began to shake up the crumpled cushions on the sofa. She didn't look at him. She said, 'At one time she used to have these nightmares quite often. Ever since her father died. She found his death—traumatic. I was told she would grow out of them, and she—seemed to be. She hasn't had one for ages. I'm afraid that—being round men for any length of time has tended to—trigger them in the past.'

'Then it's my fault?'

'It's no one's fault, although naturally, I try and protect her whenever possible,' She paused. 'It's all right, when it's just the two of us.'

'Is it now?' he came back at her grimly. 'So you're going to cut yourself off from normal human contact for the rest of your life to protect Jodie from nightmares? To hell with that. If Jodie needs help, then she must have it. But this isn't helping, Cass, although it may furnish you with a ready excuse for keeping the rest of the world out,' he added harshly.

She walked to the door, and opened it. 'Go,' she said. 'Just go. I don't need your help, Rohan, or your patronage, or your advice. It would be better for Jodie, better for both of us, if you just—kept away.'

'Is it that resemblance you once mentioned?' he asked, his eyes hard. 'Do I remind her of him, Cass? Is that the reason for tonight's trauma?'

Cass shook her head. 'I don't know. But you're not good for her, Rohan. And you're not good for me. I want my life back the way it was, and I'll have it, even if it means leaving the agency to get away from you. There must be some corner somewhere where your shadow can't touch me.'

In a shattering silence, he picked up his jerkin, shrugged it on, and walked past her, out of the door. Out of her life.

Tremblingly, she closed the door, locked it, put on the chain, then leaned against its thick panels, trying to steady her breathing.

Safe, she thought. Safe at last.

And shivered, because she now knew how tenuous and fragile her whole notion of security really was.

CHAPTER FIVE

'THE trouble is,' Serena Vance said plaintively, 'I'm simply not used to this kind of commercialism. I've been used to working with truly creative people.'

She smiled wistfully around, appealing to each of the men in turn, but letting her eyes slide dismissively over Cass, who sat at the corner of the table doodling absently in her notebook.

Roger cleared his throat. 'I'm sure we're all aware of your difficulties, Miss Vance, and we do sympathise. But the fact is the shooting of this *Moonglow* commercial should have been wrapped up yesterday. And the director does have other commitments, and our studio time is limited too.'

He didn't actually say, 'Time is money' but the words seemed to hung unspoken round the room.

Serena shrugged perfect shoulders, rising from the deeply shirred frill which adorned the low cut bodice of her midnight blue taffeta evening gown. 'Darlings, I'm so sorry,' she apologised charmingly. 'But I'm sure, with a few adjustments, the script could work quite well.'

Cass said quietly, 'A number of changes have been made already, Miss Vance. It's difficult to see what other areas we can move into without getting right away from the product image we're trying to project.'

Serena shuddered elaborately. 'All that terrible jargon, Ms Linton. Is it any wonder we're having problems. We simply don't speak the same language.'

Cass smiled faintly. 'And yet the *Sundance* ad went quite smoothly,' she pointed out.

There was an electric silence. The shooting for the commercial had gone through without a hitch, because at that time Serena had not been aware that Cass was largely responsible for the script, and there wasn't a soul in the room unaware of the fact, including Serena herself.

Serena's eyes were wintry. She looked Cass over slowly and deliberately, letting her eyes linger on the dull beige cotton jeans, and the matching battledress top.

She said kindly, 'Ms Linton, a woman's perfume should be an extension of her personality—intimate, sensuous, glamorous. I'm wondering if you can genuinely empathise with such concepts. You tend, my dear, to be rather— an unvarnished little person, if you'll forgive my saying so,' she added with a little laugh.

There was a stunned silence. Cass's pencil dug into the pad, breaking its point, but her own smile didn't waver.

She said, 'But I do have one distinct advantage, Miss Vance. What I lack in surface gloss, I make up in imagination. And now I'll put that imagination to work on formulating some lines that you will be able to manage. Excuse me.'

She got up and walked out of the room, resisting the impulse to slam the door behind her. It occurred to her she might also have walked out of a job, but she would worry about that later, she thought tiredly. It might be worth being unemployed if she no longer had to submit to the kind of smiling malice Serena Vance had subjected her to. But Cass could have put up with all the barbs coming her way while they were on a personal level only. It was when her professional capabilities were being attacked that the real problems started, with Serena deliberately and sweetly ruining take after take with her protests about the lines she had to say.

Tony Gregory, the director, had summed up the situation gloomily the day before. 'The woman's pure bitch,' he's said morosely. 'But she's magic when you turn a lens on her, and she could sell snow to the North Pole if she put her mind to it, and if we can just get her working properly, both these commercials are going to be a sensation.'

The best thing she could do, Cass thought, would be to 'phone Barney and ask to be taken off the account, and a man appointed in her place.

But Barney would not hear of it when she spoke to him a few minutes later.

'She's only a bloody actress,' he bellowed in disgust. 'Tell Gregory to pull her into line.'

'He handles her very well,' Cass told him wearily. 'It's just myself she objects to, and I'm sure if I wasn't there, things would improve.'

Barney's rich chuckle reached her. 'Defeated by a rag, a bone and a hank of hair, Cass? That's not like you. What's happened to my gutsy woman?' He paused. 'But don't panic. I'll send some cavalry.'

What indeed had happened to her, Cass wondered, as she emerged from the 'phone booth. The fight seemed to have gone out of her, and although she'd blamed post-flu depression when colleagues exclaimed concernedly over her wan looks and listlessness, she couldn't cite this indefinitely.

And she knew what ailed her, if she was honest with herself. She'd made herself face it during one sleepless night after another. She'd sent Rohan Grant out of her life for good, and his departure had left an aching void of loneliness which no amount of work, or frenetic activity in her leisure moments could fill.

Jodie, bewildered but appreciative, had found herself taken relentlessly round museums and art galleries, as well as visiting the Tower and sailing down the Thames to Greenwich. Lloyd had accompanied them a couple of times, with reasonable success, Cass thought frowning a little, although Jodie hadn't reacted to him with the same instinctive warmth as she'd shown Rohan Grant. But then, she hadn't had any nightmares since either.

Cass had never thought she would ever be grateful for Jodie having a nightmare, yet she had to admit in her secret heart that last bad dream had been totally fortuitous, dragging her back from the brink of surrender. She burned whenever she thought of it, of herself going quietly crazy with desire in Rohan's arms after all her protestations. The biggest pushover in the history of the world, she thought disgustedly. But if Rohan had woken the sleeping fires within her, she'd managed to dampen them again quite successfully, and Lloyd had never tempted her to allow them to be rekindled. He was—nice, she thought with a mental shrug, but she would

never tremble with passion in his arms, or wait
with desperate joy for him to remove her clothes.

How Lloyd might view the situation, of course,
might be a different matter. If she read the signs,
he wasn't looking for friendly threesomes, but a
relationship, and she had nothing to offer him.

With an effort she tore her mind back to the
subject of *Moonglow* perfume, and the despised
script. She would have to make further changes,
she thought wrily. She had little choice. And she
was thankful she had not been forced to do the
same thing with the *Sundance* copy.

Moonglow, she thought, mysterious and seductive. It was hard to know what other line to
pursue. The colour and style of Serena's dress
seemed right, and so did the setting, a formal
garden with tall hedges, statuary and a marble
bench, all bathed in moonlight. And at the end
the shadowy figure of an unknown man, his hand
touching her bare shoulder, bending to caress the
side of her neck with his lips. All very sultry and
evocative, and Serena had been enthusiastic
about it until she'd actually discovered who'd
been responsible for creating that romantic and
seductive scene.

Cass sighed. She and Miss Vance had not set
eyes on each other since that night at the theatre,
and she'd hoped against hope that the actress
might have forgotten all about her. And at first
Serena hadn't seemed to recognise her, now that
Cass had reverted with a vengeance to her drab
gear and hairstyle. She'd kept a deliberately low
profile too when she was on the set, letting Roger
make any suggestions which were needed. But all,
ultimately, to no avail. Serena had known exactly

who she was from the first, Cass admitted ruefully. There'd come a moment when she'd glanced up and seen the actress looking at her with exactly the same expression as her beautiful face had worn when she'd found Cass alone with Rohan, and deep in what was clearly a personal conversation, at the end of the theatre interval.

I should have gone to Barney then, she thought, and asked to be allowed to fade into total obscurity. This whole commercial would be wrapped up and in the can by now.

She sighed, and began to walk slowly back to the studio, head bent.

A voice said bitingly, 'Risking another collision, Cass?'

She looked up with a gasp, to see Rohan blocking her way. It was the first time she'd seen him since he'd walked out of the flat that night, and she felt that terrible hidden hunger uncurl into gnawing life as her eyes met his.

She swallowed. 'What are you doing here?'

'Not chasing you, so forget the panic,' he said curtly. 'Finiston tells me there are problems, and I find that's an under-estimation. Gregory says there hasn't been a single decent take for two days.'

'That's quite true.' She kept her voice level. 'I'm afraid Miss Vance and I seem to be having a clash of personalities.'

'I heard that too,' he came back at her grimly. 'You specialise in clashing, don't you, Ms Linton, and not just in your private life either.'

'You're saying it's all my fault?' She stared up at him, her lips parted in indignation.

He shrugged. 'I wasn't here, so I can't

apportion blame. But—she's the star, Cass, and you're the agency girl. If one of you has to bend, I think it should be you. If Serena wants a line rewritten, then do your bloody job, and rewrite it, and let's stop wasting time and money.'

She looked at him for a long bitter moment, then took a deep breath. 'Oh, yes, sir. Three bags full, *sir*. Would you like me to humbly apologise to the lady too for my actual existence?'

'That won't be necessary,' he told her grimly. 'I'm here now, and I'm staying until Gregory gets every line from you, and every shot from her that he wants. And after that, it might be better if Finiston puts you on to another assignment altogether. We don't want any more unfortunate—clashes.'

'That suits me ideally,' Cass said, a bright spot of colour glowing in either cheek. 'I only hope Barney agrees with you.'

'He will,' Rohan said coldly and succinctly. 'And now could you stop wandering around the place, brooding over your wrongs, and get together with Roger to see what you can salvage from the original script.'

He turned on his heel and walked away, leaving her to follow in his wake. She was shaking with temper, but she forced herself to a semblance of composure before going back in the studio. She wanted no-one—and Serena Vance in particular—to see that she was upset.

Roger almost leaped at her. 'Cass? Where have you been?' He pulled her into a corner. 'Grant's here,' he muttered. 'He's been stalking round the place giving orders like Jove's thunderbolts. Even La Vance hasn't dared open her mouth for twenty minutes. It must be a record.'

'I've seen him,' Cass said wearily. 'We have to placate the lady with a new script which will appeal to her basic artistry.'

'He ought to try placating her himself,' Roger said with a faint leer. 'That's what she wants. She can hardly keep her hands off him as it is.'

'Then perhaps you'd like to suggest it to him,' Cass said too evenly.

He shuddered. 'No thanks.' He gave her a weak smile. 'Maybe we should just have another look at the script. Before the next thunderbolt hits us.'

In the event thay had more time and more privacy than they expected, because Tony Gregory called an early lunch break, and Cass saw an openly triumphant Serena, changed into her day clothes, being led off by Rohan Grant.

'They're probably going to have *filet mignon* while we make do with cheese sandwiches and coffee,' Roger said mournfully. He brightened. 'Hey—maybe she'll get a bad prawn in her cocktail. I had one once, and I thought I was going to die, I can tell you.'

'You did tell me—several times,' Cass gave him a reluctant grin. 'But it's a nice idea—and then we could get nice, harmless, amenable Tracey back.'

By the time Serena returned resplendent and glowing from lunch, and whatever had preceded or followed it, they had finished.

And Serena, as she soon made clear, was in the mood to be pleased.

'Oh, that's much better,' she exclaimed as she read the new lines. She gave Cass a patronising look. 'So, you can do it, Ms Linton, when you try. This is infinitely superior to your earlier efforts—so much more drama, so much more depth—and—and erotic intensity than before.'

Cass's brows lifted. 'I thought we were writing a popular scent commercial,' she said. 'Not the remake of *Gone with the Wind*.'

Towering above his companion, Rohan gave Cass a grim look, but before he could say anything, Tony Gregory hastily intervened. 'Well, how about a run-through to make sure the moves are absolutely right. Serena—if you'd like to change.'

They all began to move off, to make final adjustments to the set, and prepare for the next take. Cass was left alone with Rohan.

He said softly, icily, 'That beautiful mouth is going to talk you into real trouble one of these days, Ms Linton.'

She said wearily, 'I think I already have all the trouble I can handle. But not having to see you again will be one load of mischief the less.'

His eyes narrowed. 'How's Jodie?'

'Very well, thank you,' she returned levelly.

'No more bad dreams?'

She stiffened slightly. 'Fortunately, no.'

'Another blessing brought about by my departure?' The hazel eyes held hers, and it was an effort to tear her gaze away.

She shrugged. 'You said it. I didn't,' she returned shortly.

He said, 'James and Simon have been asking about her. It's getting close to Easter. My sister was wondering whether you would let her invite Jodie down to Graystocks for a few days.'

'That's out of the question,' Cass said sharply.

'It doesn't have to be.' His mouth curled

slightly. 'After all, under other circumstances you might both have been spending Easter in the country with me.'

With a calmness that was far from genuine, she said, 'I don't think so. I'm sure you'd have been tired of me by this time.' She paused. 'Besides— you have a prior commitment—to Miss Vance.'

'How good of you to remind me,' he drawled. 'I also, if you remember, made certain promises to your beautiful daughter which I am anxious to redeem. And what I said to you before still stands, Cass. The child needs masculine company. That feminine hothouse you're rearing her in isn't going to give her the balanced outlook on life she needs, or stop the nightmares for good,' he added grimly. 'It's incredible to me that so young a child could have been so badly affected by her father's death. I'd have thought she was barely old enough to remember him at all.'

Cass had to force herself to stand her ground. There was a faint roaring in her ears, and she had to breathe deeply. She said swiftly and briefly, 'Brett was—killed in a road accident. Jodie witnessed it. Is that sufficient explanation?'

'It's obviously all I'm going to get,' he said bitterly. 'All right, Cass, have it your way.'

'I know what's best for my own child,' she said angrily. 'And she has plenty of masculine company. I—I'm seeing Lloyd regularly now. She's growing to—to accept his presence around the flat quite naturally.'

'Including overnight?'

There was a note in his voice which spelled danger. Her hands hidden in the pockets of her jeans, Cass crossed her fingers surreptitiously.

'Yes,' she said recklessly.

'I see.' His drawl lengthened. 'Doesn't having Jodie around all the time cramp his style a little, or have you trained him to confine his ardour discreetly to the bedroom, and only when she's asleep?'

'That's none of your damned business,' Cass said hotly.

He smiled unpleasantly. 'Oh, but I'm fascinated, sweetheart. Having—almost—shared Haswell's good fortune, that is. Do you like your pleasures tame and domesticated, Cass? I thought you'd be a wild one—once you'd shaken off that tight rein you had on yourself.' He gave her an insolent look. 'How does Haswell like your present wardrobe? Or does he work on the principle that the uglier a woman's clothes, the more pleasure there is in taking them off?'

Cass bit her lip until she tasted blood. She said, 'Can we stop right there please? I find this—speculation about my sexuality thoroughly distasteful.'

'Oh really,' he said. 'And I find the thought of you with Haswell equally so.' He gave her a derisive look. 'There's a thought to take to bed with you next time. It should add an extra—piquancy to the encounter, shall we say?'

'I'd prefer you not to say anything more,' she said raggedly. 'Anything at all.' She looked past him. 'And your—mistress is waiting for you.'

'Is she?' His eyes never left her face. 'What a sweet old fashioned term for a committed feminist to use. You make her sound as if I keep her in a little place in St John's Wood and shower her with jewels and furs.'

'Starting with a mink cloak.' The words were out before she knew it.

He laughed. 'Oh, I'm capable of the odd generous gesture,' he said. 'And you must admit she looked good in it. The photographs were fantastic—especially those that weren't for publication. In fact, she's a magnificent lady in every way, and you're quite right—I shouldn't keep her waiting.'

She stood by herself, staring down at the papers she was holding while the words danced in a meaningless jumble in front of her eyes. Her legs felt weak and there was an agonisingly hollow feeling in the pit of her stomach.

Roger joined her. 'Keep your fingers crossed,' he said in a low voice. 'Tony's having one run-through, then going for a take. Let's hope that Sarah Bernhardt behaves this time.'

'Where's Peter?' Serena was demanding imperiously, seeking the actor who was to play the unknown man joining her at the end of the commercial. 'I need him here.'

'He's popped up to make-up for a minute,' Tony said soothingly. 'One of the lads will walk it through with you, if that's what you want.'

'Rohan.' Serena gave him the full treatment, eyes shining, lips pouting provocatively. 'You do it, darling.' She gave a tinkling laugh. 'It is only a run-through after all. Equity won't object.'

Rohan shrugged slightly. 'Why not?'

A moment later, Cass found herself watching the transformation of Serena Vance. A woman, she thought, her eyes full of secret dreams, perfumed and alluring, awaiting the arrival of her lover in the moonlight. Exactly what they'd

wanted from the start, and who cared about the
words she was saying. All the millions who'd
eventually watch the commercial would remember would be that lovely, erotic face, and the
husky-throated tones promising them paradise.

'*Moonglow*' Serena said softly, sinking down on
to her bench. 'The start of your own very
personal magic.'

Rohan stepped forward, and put his hand on
her shoulder, stroking away the frill. Then he
bent without haste and put his mouth against her
long white throat, and Serena gasped ecstatically
tipping her head back against his shoulder.

For a moment there was total, almost shocked
silence, then Rohan lifted his head, moved, and a
semblance of normality returned.

Beside Cass, Roger emitted a long, low whistle.
'Parental Guidance only,' he muttered. 'My God,
they should forget about the scent, and bottle
what's between those two instead. They'd make a
fortune.'

Cass didn't speak. A long shudder went
through her. Seeing Rohan touch Serena, kiss her
throat, had filled her with an anguish so intense
she had nearly cried out.

Across the studio, Rohan's gaze searched for
hers, locked with hers, in fierce, cynical triumph.

She looked back numbly, knowing that he'd
see what she had been unable to hide in time.
Knowing that he'd recognised the fact that he
could make her suffer.

There was no shelter for her to cower behind
any more. No pretended indifference to guard
her. He'd seen her—exposed, vulnerable, jealous—and now he knew all he needed to know.

Somehow she pulled herself together, and turned to Roger, forcing a smile. 'Then let's pray she can produce the same reaction with poor old Peter, so we can all go home.'

Home, she thought. To a flat with sunshine walls, and shadows that waited in the night.

The take which followed was perfect. Serena, wreathed in smiles, was congratulated by everyone. Cass watched her turn to Rohan, lift her face for his kiss, and turned away, realising as she did so, that the pencil between her tense fingers had snapped completely in half.

Rohan was speaking again, and she forced herself to listen.

'Thank you all for a good professional job,' he said. 'I'm having a party at my house in the country in two weeks' time to celebrate the launch of the whole campaign, and naturally, you are all invited, although my secretary will be in touch with more formal invitations.'

'Well, that's generous,' Roger muttered. 'Just what I've always wanted. A chance to see how the other half lives.'

She managed a quick, bright smile. 'I hope you enjoy it.'

'Well, you'll be there too,' he said, giving her a surprised look.

She shook her head. 'I doubt if I'll be invited. I'm being taken off the account by Mr Grant's special request.'

Roger's dismayed expression would have been heartwarming, if she'd been in the mood to appreciate it.

'The bastard,' he said indignantly. 'I thought you seemed to be having a pretty fraught conversation with him just now. Was that what it was all about?'

'It was—related,' Cass said neutrally. 'But don't get me wrong, Roger. If Mr Grant hadn't suggested that I stop working on *Eve*, then I would have done. It's been bad news from the start, as far as I'm concerned.'

'Hm.' Roger gave her a considering look. 'I don't want to pry, Cass, but I remember the last time we talked about this. Is it a personal thing?'

She bit her lip. 'You could say so.'

He groaned. 'Oh, Cassie. I tried to warn you.' He paused awkwardly. 'If you want a shoulder to cry on, then Lorna . . .'

She interrupted gently. 'Thanks, Roger, but fortunately, there's nothing to cry over.'

But was that really true? she asked herself. Hadn't she been crying inside for weeks now?

Roger patted her shoulder. 'That's all right then. Work's the thing,' he went on. 'After all, you've got to be realistic in this life, and you— and a guy like Rohan Grant?' He shook his head decisively. 'Never in a month of Sundays.'

No, never, Cass thought when she was alone. Never—in all the long bleak months which lay ahead.

CHAPTER SIX

WORK, Cass discovered in the days which
followed, could be an anodyne, but it didn't
dissolve the pain completely.

She was bewildered by the strength of her own
feelings. After Brett, she had lived with the
conviction that there never would—never could
be another man in her life.

Now she knew differently, and the fact that the
man in question only wanted her for his own
casual sexual gratification hadn't even blunted
the pang of the sharp, shattering desire she
experienced each time she thought of him.

She'd never realised she was capable of such
emotion. Nothing in her short, tragic marriage
had prepared her for such a revelation. In fact,
she'd always believed she was frigid, and blamed
this, to some extent, for the terrible failure of her
relationship with Brett. It was the same conviction
which had made her retreat into her shell,
camouflage her femininity, and follow the path of
self-sufficiency, telling herself that one disaster
was enough. As a burned child fears the fire,
she'd shrunk from the prospect of any kind of
intimacy with a man.

But why—oh, why did it have to be Rohan
Grant who'd woken her from her drugged,
isolated sleep, and taught her that her numbed
body, her dazed crushed senses had responses—
needs she'd never even imagined?

Because the most she could hope for from him was a brief surcease to the cravings which assailed her. A fix for her addiction, she thought wretchedly.

And she didn't want that—to live her life at the mercy of her body's needs. Because when Rohan tired of her—as he inevitably would—what then?

No, she told herself vehemently, it was better this way. Better to live with a hunger which would never be satisfied than to feed it with crumbs.

There was Lloyd, of course. A smile of self-derision twisted her lips. The safe half-loaf, she thought, hating herself, that everyone said was better than no bread at all. Only she'd never believed that, and never would.

She was seeing too much of Lloyd, using him as a palliative, with the result that he was now beginning to regard himself as a fixture in her life, making plans which she didn't want to share, making references to the future which worried her. No, she hadn't been fair to Lloyd.

And he'd nearly hit the roof when he discovered she wasn't going to the party at Graystocks, the Grants' country home. She'd torn the card, when it arrived, into very tiny pieces, and buried them at the bottom of her waste basket, before returning a brief formal refusal.

'But you must go,' he'd almost howled. 'Everyone's going. After all the man's an important client. Does Barney know about this?'

Cass shrugged. 'It's impossible for me to go,' she said evasively. 'As it happens, Mrs Barrett's sister has her silver wedding party that same evening, and so I have no sitter for Jodie. And even Barney would hardly expect me to go out and leave her alone, even for *Eve* cosmetics.'

'Surely there are other sitters,' he protested sullenly.

She sighed. 'Thousands, I expect, but I'm not prepared to leave Jodie with strangers either. I'm sorry, but that's the way it is.'

He chewed his lips frustratedly. 'Well, it's a damned nuisance. My parents don't live far from Graystocks, and I'd half-arranged for us to spend the night there so they could meet you.'

'Then perhaps you should have consulted me first.' She saw him look downcast and said more kindly, 'There'll be other occasions, Lloyd, if you want me to meet them.'

'Yes, but this time we'd have been on our own,' he muttered.

'Without Jodie, do you mean?' Cass gave him a straight look.

'Well, yes,' he said rather fretfully. 'You've got to understand, Cassie. Mother knows you're a widow, and she can accept that, but a widow with a ready-made family is a big step for her.'

It was a step which the unknown Mrs Haswell would never be called on to make, Cass thought without regret.

She was startled out of her reverie by the buzz of the telephone at her elbow. She picked up the receiver. 'Cass Linton.'

'Otherwise known as Jodie's mother.' A woman's voice, cool, pleasant and amused. 'How do you do, Mrs Linton? I'm Marcia Wainwright and I was wondering whether you'd possibly had second thoughts about allowing Jodie to spend a few days with us at Graystocks. It's Easter next weekend, and the boys have acquired a pony which they're dying to show her.'

Cass swallowed. 'I'm sorry,' she said stiltedly. 'It's—quite out of the question.'

'Because of the nightmares?' Mrs Wainwright asked. 'I understand your anxiety, believe me, but I can promise you she'll be well looked after. Our elderly nanny still lives with us here, and she's in seventh heaven to have something like a nursery functioning again. Neither Rohan nor I were ever allowed to have nightmares when we were small. Nanny didn't believe in them.' She paused. 'And she's dying to have another little girl to look after, as she keeps telling me. Well, I have no plans to oblige her at the moment, so it's all up to Jodie.'

Cass bit her lip. 'Mrs Wainwright, I'm sure you mean to be kind, but it isn't possible, please believe me.'

A little sigh came down the line. 'It's Rohan, isn't it?' Marcia Wainwright asked almost resignedly. 'My dynamic, attractive bastard of a brother. From his few, brief, and very guarded remarks about you, I gather you must be the first woman to turn him down since he left prep. school. My congratulations. I wonder if the Guinness Book of Records would be interested.'

Cass was startled into laughter. 'Mrs Wainwright . . .'

'Oh, Marcia, please. And I'll call you Cassie, even though we seem destined to remain apart.' She paused. 'Is that short for Cassandra, by the way?'

Cass's hand clenched round the receiver until the knuckles showed white suddenly. She said evenly, 'Yes, but I never use the name.'

'Then I won't either,' Marcia said comfortably. 'Cassie—this is silly. I could do with some stimulating female companionship, and I'm sure Jodie needs playmates. What child ever didn't? And we could always fix a time when Rohan was in London, so you didn't have to see him, if you didn't want to.' She paused again. 'If you have no transport, I could have you met at the station.'

Cass said ruefully, 'You make it very difficult for me to refuse without sounding positively ungracious, but I have to, just the same.'

'I won't pretend I'm not disappointed,' Marcia said. 'But I still have hopes of persuading you. We'll talk about it at the party tomorrow night. I look forward to meeting you.' And she rang off.

Cass replaced her receiver thoughtfully. In spite of herself, she'd liked the sound of Marcia, and Jodie often wistfully mentioned James and Simon. But it was impossible. The last person on earth she needed to be on friendly terms with was Rohan Grant's sister.

Cass breathed a sigh of relief when she reached home the following evening. The party that night seemed to have been the sole topic of conversation at the agency all day long, but fortunately her own silence on the subject seemed to have passed un-noticed.

'We're going to have a wonderfully lazy evening,' she told Jodie, as she added seasoning to a dish of chicken provencale, and put it into the oven to cook slowly. 'While we're waiting for supper, we'll have our baths and wash our hair, then eat in our dressing gowns.'

Jodie welcomed the idea with rapture. It wasn't a very relaxing bath, and shampoo and water seemed to get everywhere, but it was great fun, and Cass felt more lighthearted than she'd done for days, as she wielded the hairdryer and brush, and scented the fragrance of the casserole beginning to drift through from the kitchen.

The abrupt buzz at the front door was a totally unwelcome intrusion.

'You said a rude word,' Jodie accused.

'I did,' Cass admitted ruefully. 'I wasn't expecting callers, that's all. Perhaps if we keep very quiet, they'll go away.'

But the buzzer sounded again, more imperatively than ever. Then a longer burst, as if whoever was outside was leaning on the thing, Cass thought resentfully, as she got up to answer it, tigtening the belt of her robe as she did so.

She released the catch, and almost as she did so, Rohan walked in. She gasped and fell back, as the hazel eyes blazed down at her.

'Good evening,' he said in a silky tone which didn't fool her for an instant. 'I've just learned that you're not coming to the party tonight. May I ask why not?'

Cass looked at him incredulously. 'You've come all the way from Graystocks to ask me that?'

'Of course not,' he said. 'I'm just on my way down there now, and I'm taking you with me.' His eyes swept over her assessingly. 'Well you're half ready at least. Go and put a dress on.'

'I'll do nothing of the sort,' Cass said between her teeth.

'Is Mummy going to a party?' Jodie demanded. 'Can I go too?'

'No,' Cass said desperately. She turned to Rohan. 'I refused the invitation because Mrs Barrett has another engagement tonight, although why I should have to offer an explanation for my decision . . .'

He turned to her, smiling, his eyes glinting dangerously, looking, she thought, almost golden—tiger's eyes.

'Then you should have let us know, Cassie,' he said smoothly. 'Every problem has its solution, after all, and Jodie's suggested her own. She can go with us—and stay for a few days too. I'll ring Graystocks and warn Nanny she has a visitor.'

'Oh, Rohan—may I?' Jodie's face was transfigured.

'No,' Cass almost shouted. 'I won't hear of it.'

Rohan put a hand on Jodie's shoulder and pushed her gently towards the bedrooms. 'Go and choose all the clothes you like best,' he directed gently. 'Mummy will be in to help you presently.'

When they were alone, Cass said stormily, 'You can go to hell. I won't be pushed around by you.'

He said harshly, 'I haven't even started pushing yet. I wouldn't have known you weren't going to this party if Marcia hadn't got a guest list from my secretary and checked the names. You're one of the guests of honour and you know it, and you're not insulting me by failing to turn up. Does Finiston know you weren't planning to be there?'

'No,' she said defiantly. 'Nor do I see what difference it makes, considering I don't even work on the account any more. And while we're on the subject of guest of honour, what's Miss Vance going to say if I turn up.'

'Very little,' he said briefly. 'She's in California. Did her well publicised departure escape your notice?'

'It must have done,' she said. 'But it makes no difference. I'm still not going.'

'Oh, but you are,' he said grimly. 'Now, go and dress.'

She stamped her foot. 'No.'

He shrugged off the light overcoat he was wearing. In the formality of dinner jacket and black tie, he looked sensational, stunningly attractive, and she felt her stomach lurch crazily as she looked at him.

He strode past her, towards her bedroom, and she went after him, nearly tripping over the hem of her robe. When she caught up with him, he was standing in front of her open wardrobe, scanning impatiently along the rail.

He said, 'Your decent clothes shine out like good deeds in a sinful world.' He pulled the dress she'd worn to the theatre off its hanger and tossed it to her. 'Wear this.'

'When hell freezes over.'

He smiled charmingly. 'Then I'll put the bloody thing on you myself. Believe me, it will be my pleasure.'

He moved towards her, his eyes going to the belt of her robe. Beneath the thin fabric, she was naked, and they both knew it.

She whispered shakily, 'No' and put out a hand to fend him away. 'No—please.' She swallowed. 'I'll do it.'

He nodded. 'I'll sort Jodie out,' he said

expressionlessly and left her.

Moving like an automaton, she found a handful of underwear, and began to put it on, hastily covering herself with the dress in case he came back to check on her progress. She sank down on the stool in front of her dressing table and stared at herself. Her eyes looked enormous—like a bush baby's in the pallor of her face. Fumbling a little, she began to apply moisturiser and foundation. A mask, she thought, to hide behind, and never had she needed one more.

She was clumsy with the eye shadow and had to wipe it off and start again, taking slow deep breaths to calm herself. Her hand was surer with the blusher and mascara wand, and she etched in the contours of her mouth in colour with barely a tremor.

The car, waiting for them in the street below, was low, sleek and frighteningly powerful. Cass stopped looking at the speedometer after a while, although she had to admit Rohan was a first class driver. He didn't speak, and neither did she, yet their awareness of each other seemed total. And that was frightening too—hurtling through the darkness in this enforced intimacy while Jodie drowsed on the back seat. In some strange way it was one of the most disturbing things which had ever happened to her.

At last she felt she had to break the silence, or scream. She said, 'Won't your guests be wondering where you are?'

He shrugged slightly. 'Marcia knows I may be late and why,' he said. 'She can cope, and she has the rest of the *Eve* board to help her.'

Cass shook her head helplessly. 'Why have you

done this?' she asked quietly. 'You couldn't wait
to get me off the account.'

'I couldn't wait to get you out of my particular
orbit,' he came back at her grimly. 'Only, it isn't
as simple as that—is it?'

Cass looked down at her hands clenched
together in her lap. 'No,' she admitted dully.

He made a small sound in his throat, but
whether it was prompted by satisfaction or
exasperation, she could not tell.

Graystocks was a big Georgian manor, floodlit
from the drive and gardens, and with additional
light spilling from the windows and open front
door. Cars, she noticed, were still arriving.

Rohan drove round to the side of the house and
through an arched gateway into a large cobbled
yard where he stopped. He said, 'I'm sorry this is
the back way, but it will make it easier to find
Nanny for Jodie.' Moving gently so as not to
disturb the dozing child, he lifted her from the
rear of the car, then walked with her into the
house, while Cass followed.

The domestic area of the house seemed vast to
Cass, used to one small kitchenette, and crowded
with people. She found herself wondering how
many were permanent staff, and how many
merely hired for the evening. Rohan led the way,
regardless of the bustle going on around him, to a
door opening on to a steep flight of stairs.

Nanny, a tall, rather gaunt woman with a
serene face, was waiting at the top of the stairs.

'Good evening, sir,' she said calmly. She sent
Cass an appraising glance. 'And good evening to
you, madam. If you could bring the little girl
along, we'll pop her into bed.' She sent Cass a

peculiarly sweet smile as if she divined her inner unrest. 'There's really no need to worry about her. She'll be safe here.'

As Cass murmured her thanks, Rohan appeared again. 'We'll go downstairs,' he ordained abruptly. 'You can check on her later, if you wish.'

'Of course I wish,' she retorted, nettled. She bit her lip. 'I suppose you think I'm being over-fussy, but she has had problems—and she's all I've got,' she added defensively.

He sent her an ironic look, but his voice was politely expressionless as he said, 'Of course.'

A tidal wave of noise seemed to flow towards them as they emerged from the nursery wing, and walked along a broad gallery towards the main staircase. Cass could hear the throb of disco music mixed with the buzz of voices and laughter, and nervousness swept over her. Joining the party in the company of the master of the house was not her idea of an unobtrusive entrance. She hung back slightly, pretending to examine some of the portraits on the walls. One in particular caught her eye, and she stared at it, her interest real. The subject was a tall woman, her hair swept up into one of the elaborate styles which preceded the Great War, her slender throat circled by a pearl choker. She was beautiful, but it was the serene laughter in her eyes which gave the portrait its character.

'My grandmother,' Rohan said. 'The Eve after whom the cosmetic company was named. I told you once it was dear to my heart, and now you know why.' He added mockingly, 'I do have these occasional flashes of humanity.'

It was a side of him she would prefer not to be aware of, Cass thought, turning blindly away without replying.

She was bitterly aware of the curious glances coming her way as she descended the staircase by Rohan's side.

'So you made it.' It was a girl's voice amused and satisfied, and Cass turned abruptly to find herself being confronted by someone tall with brown hair and hazel eyes, and a familiarly lazy grin curving her mouth.

'Yes, we are alike, aren't we?' she said cordially as if Cass had spoken. 'But,' she lowered her voice. 'I wouldn't let my predatory brother see you gaping like that or he might think all hope was not dead.' She held out her hand. 'Jodie, I presume, is already dead to the world upstairs. I look forward to making her acquaintance tomorrow. You are going to let her stay?'

Cass said stiffly, 'It seems so. I was given little choice.'

Marcia laughed. 'A family trait, I'm afraid. I hope you'll forgive us for steamrollering you like this. But I'm sure it will be good for her, and marvellous for the boys. I suppose I can't persuade you to be our guest too.'

'I'm afraid not.'

Marcia sighed. 'I was afraid of that too,' she acknowledged with a rueful grin. She was wearing a black dress which had probably cost a month of Cass's salary, and a string of exquisite pearls. 'Now, what can I get you to drink?'

Cass opted for white wine, and as Marcia turned away to signal an approaching waitress,

Lloyd's voice said thunderously, 'I thought you said you weren't coming.'

'I wasn't,' Cass returned levelly. 'But it would take too long to explain.

And explanations could be complicated, she thought with a little inward shiver. Everything was moving too fast suddenly, sweeping her inexorably along paths she could not comprehend.

He looked explosive. 'But I would have brought you,' he protested. 'How did you get here?'

She sighed. 'Rohan brought me.'

He looked totally nonplussed. 'But didn't you explain about the kid?'

Several times,' she said with forced gaiety. 'As a matter of fact, she's here too, asleep upstairs.'

Lloyd was looking at her as if she'd just grown an extra head. 'It all seems very cosy,' he said at last. 'How long have you been on these kind of terms with the Grants.'

'I haven't, and I'm not,' she said wearily. 'It was just—a way out of an impasse, that's all. And, as it happens, Jodie did meet the Wainwright boys once, and they've asked her to spend a few days here.'

While he was absorbing that, Marcia reappeared. 'Your drink,' she said to Cassie then awarded Lloyd one of her candid smiles. 'Hello, I don't think we've met. I'm Marcia Wainwright. You're not dancing, and you're not eating, and you must do one or the other. Let me introduce you round a little.'

Lloyd gaped at her as if she'd popped up through the floorboards in a puff of smoke. 'Haswell,' he muttered. 'Lloyd Haswell.'

Marcia beckoned, and a pretty blonde whom Cass recognised from her modelling work with the agency, joined them smilingly.

'Hattie, darling,' Marcia cooed. 'Do take Lloyd somewhere and make him smile again. I'm sure you can.'

Hattie slid a hand through his arm. 'I'm starving,' she told him plaintively.

Lloyd submitted and allowed himself to be led away, mouthing 'I'll talk to you later,' at Cass.

'Oh, dear,' Marcia said. 'The boyfriend?'

'Not really,' Cass said soberly. 'Just—a friend.' But for how much longer, she asked herself. Lloyd had the air of a man with a grievance, and perhaps it was a genuine one, although she'd tried to make the limits of their relationship clear to him.

'Cassie.' Barney's genial version of his usual bellow assaulted her ears, and he came over to her. 'Having a good time? Sal and I were looking for you earlier.'

'She only just got here,' Marcia said blandly. 'Special delivery,' she added as she drifted away again.

'Quite a lady,' Barney said approvingly, watching her retreating figure. 'If this campaign is a success, and we get more work from Grants, then may be I can get Sal a string of pearls like that.'

More people joined them, and the group around them began to expand. Grateful for Barney's wing to shelter under, Cass started to relax, and even, as time passed, to enjoy herself. She ate her way through a huge plateful of delicious food, drank more wine, and danced hilariously to the disco, sometimes in a crowd, sometimes with individual partners.

She danced once with Lloyd who was clearly looking for an argument and peeved because the loudness of the music prevented him from starting one. She gently but firmly resisted his attempts to persuade her to accompany him to somewhere quieter, and was relieved to be able to refuse his sulky offer of a lift back to London by saying she'd already agreed to drive back with Barney and Sal. She didn't see him again after that, and guessed, half-guiltily that he'd taken his sense of injury home with him.

The earlier frenetic energy of the party had quietened too. People seemed to have made the contacts they needed, and the coversation and shared laughter was more muted and intimate as time moved into the small hours. Even the disco music had gentled, and couples were in each other's arms, swaying quietly to the new, slower rhythm.

Cass leaned against the wall, watching reflectively. They would be leaving soon, she thought. Sal had an *au pair*, but she was a fond and conscientious mother who never liked the children to be without her for very long. She'd been getting visibly restless for some time, although Barney was good for hours yet, Cass thought affectionately.

With a start, she realised she was no longer alone.

In the shadowy room, Rohan's face was unreadable. Without speaking he drew her on to the dance floor, his hands closing on her waist and pulling her against him.

'Hold me,' he ordered quietly, and obediently, she lifted her hands to his shoulders, moving with him to the slow beat of the music, her blood a sudden millrace in her veins.

He said, 'Are you leaving with Barney, or will you stay?'

Dry-mouthed, she said, 'I—must go.' The brush of his body against hers as they danced was an unbelievable torment. Yet he made no attempt to follow the example of the others around him and kiss her, or even hold her more intimately. She ran her tongue round her lips. 'May—may I see Jodie before I go?'

'Naturally.' He paused. 'Now?'

She nodded. 'Please.'

He turned her towards the doorway, his arm round her waist, anchoring her to his side. People spoke to them as they passed, and he responded without pausing, threading his way through the chattering groups to the stairs, apologising pleasantly for disturbing the throng who'd gone to ground there, leading Cass between them, up to the gallery and beyond.

The nursery suite was quiet and dark. Rohan looked in on the boys first. They were asleep in a tumble of pyjamaed limbs and duvets, and he paused to straighten the covers before taking Cass on to Jodie's room.

Her daughter lay on her side, her face angelic in repose, her thumb drooping between sleeping lips. Cass removed it gently, then touched Jodie's hair in a butterfly caress.

'Good night, sweetheart. See you soon,' she whispered.

Outside, the landing was in darkness, its sole

illumination the big square window, and the fierce brilliance of the stars beyond its panes.

Rohan was waiting for her there, his tall figure very still, and almost tense.

She sent to him slowly, aware of a deep inner trembling. His hands clasped her wrists, drawing her towards him. The handsome face was all planes and angles in the half-light, as he stared down at her, his eyes glittering like jewels.

She seemed to have stopped breathing when at last he bent towards her and put his mouth on hers, and her response was instant, almost stricken, her lips parting for him in yearning submission.

She heard him sigh in his throat, then he gathered her full against him, almost lifting her off her feet, so that her small breasts were crushed against the hardness of his chest while the kiss deepened—lengthened endlessly.

There was a hunger in him, a famine which she recognised because she shared it. An appetite that no kiss alone could satisfy, Cass knew as she clung to him, her slim body twisting in frustration at the layers of cloth which separated them from each other. She was silently begging to be taken and she knew it, and later she would probably die of shame remembering it, but now all she could think of was being part of him, absorbed by him—his body possessing hers as his mouth was signalling by its fiercely sensual invasion of her own.

It was physically painful when at last he lifted his head.

He said, 'They're waiting for you downstairs.'

Her nails dug into her palms as she fought to

match his calmness—his utter control. 'It—it must be very late.'

'A whole new day,' he said. He took her unresisting hand and carried it to his lips, caressing the soft palm with his lips, making sweet tremors envelop her body. He said huskily, 'Have dinner with me tonight.'

She knew, because he'd warned her once, what dimensions of intimacy the invitation covered, and reason—commonsense alone—screamed at her to be true to her first instincts about this man, and about herself, and refuse, as she'd done before. It was madness to yield—madness . . .

She whispered, 'Yes.'

He nodded. 'Eight, then,' he said almost abruptly. 'I'll send a car for you.'

His hands cupped her face for a long moment, the long fingers stroking her dishevelled hair back from her face, moving softly and sensuously over her small ears, and the sensitive areas just beneath them, soothing the pulse in her throat, as it fluttered like a small wounded bird.

When he let her go, it was with obvious reluctance. Their eyes met.

He said in stark commitment, 'Tonight.'

Cass nodded. She couldn't speak.

Barney and Sal were waiting in the hall, and all the way downstairs, Cass was conscious of Barney's brows drawn together in overt disapproval, aware of Marcia's mischievous wink as she said good night.

Rohan accompanied them out to the car, the conversation general civilities about the success of the party as he and Barney walked together. He turned to Cass last, his smile polite, his handshake conventional. Only Cass knew that his mouth had shaped, 'Tonight' instead of the usual leavetaking.

She sat in the rear seat while Barney and Sal chatted desultorily. She was blind and deaf to anything except that one word 'Tonight' echoing and re-echoing in her head.

When they reached her flat, Barney insisted on coming up with her and waiting while she opened the door.

He said abruptly, 'I hope you're not going to make a fool of yourself, Cassie.'

She tried to speak lightly. 'It seems likely. I'm—due for a little stupidity, don't you think?'

'A little, maybe,' Barney said gloomily. 'But Rohan Grant seems like foolishness on the grand scale to me.' He scowled. 'Why the hell does he have to be such an attractive bastard?' he demanded rhetorically. 'And why can't he stick to women who know the score?'

She smiled sadly. 'Perhaps he thinks I do. After all, that's the way you packaged me and presented me to him.'

'Don't remind me,' Barney patted her on the shoulder with a heavy hand. 'I think I should have left you in your Oxfam rejects.'

She went into the flat, closing the door behind her. She had a very long day to face before— tonight.

CHAPTER SEVEN

IT was the longest day she'd ever experienced. Cass couldn't settle to anything, couldn't concentrate. At moments, she wished Jodie was there. At others, she was glad she wasn't. She made herself coffee, and threw it away untouched. She creamed mushrooms on toast for her lunch, and let them burn.

In the afternoon, totally irritated with herself, she went for a walk, glancing into the shop windows as she passed with the eyes of total indifference. Except one—a boutique in a small cul de sac which she'd never even considered before because it was too expensive, and because the styles so sparingly displayed in its window, had no relevance to the life she had chosen.

Now she paused, staring at the dress on display, and telling herself how many kinds of a fool she was even to contemplate it.

Fifteen minutes later, walking home with the carrier bag, she knew she was totally insane.

It had fitted her perfectly, just as she'd known it would. The colour was deep jade green, the material the finest wool jersey, the style sleek and wrap-round, fastened with a sash. Sleeves and skirt alike were long and close-fitting, and the crossover neckline plunged deeply and dramatically almost to her waist, hinting with deliberate provocation at the soft roundness of her barely concealed breasts.

A different kind of camouflage this time, she thought, and designed to conceal her fears and inadequacies in exactly the same way as her usual drab choice of clothing had done.

God only knew whether it would succeed, she thought, panic rising sickly in her throat. Yet, she wanted him so much. Wouldn't that need be sufficient to drown the past forever?

She still wasn't sure when she went through the ritual of bathing, of scenting her body, and applying a light dusting of make up to accentuate her lips and eyes. Slowly and carefully, she applied nail enamel in a glowing pink to her finger and toenails. It was a long time since she'd taken so much trouble. The years seemed to roll back, and she was a young girl again—Cassie, dressing for a date with all her future in front of her like an unopened book.

She shivered. Only now that book had chapters. Chapters that would stay closed forever from tonight, she prayed feverishly.

When the buzzer sounded, she took one last look and reached for her wrap.

A uniformed chauffeur was waiting at the door. 'Mrs Linton?' he inquired respectfully. 'Good evening, madam. The car is waiting.'

She said quietly, 'Thank you,' and followed him down to the street.

This time it was a limousine she registered with amazement. It surrounded her in luxury, drawing her down into a comfort she had never dreamed of. She heard the man say it was chilly, and offer her a rug, which she declined.

She wondered where she was being driven, but the chauffeur hadn't volunteered the information,

and she was not prepared to ask. Presumably, she
would be supposed to know already, she told
herself drily. She guessed she would be taken to a
restaurant somewhere in the West End, with a
night club to follow. Her imagination refused to
carry her beyond that point.

The car was slowing, turning into a large
square. She looked out with bewilderment at the
row of Regency houses confronting her. If there
was a restaurant here, they were being very
discreet about it. There were no signs, or
awnings, or even a commissionaire.

As the chauffeur helped her out of the car, she
saw the door at the top of the elegant flight of
stone steps had opened and a woman in a dark
dress stood waiting to welcome her.

Fighting for composure, Cass mounted the steps.

'Good evening, Mrs Linton.' A pleasant voice
with a faint North Country burr. 'May I take
your wrap?'

Cass surrendered it in a kind of daze as she took
in her surroundings. She was in a large hall with
a tiled floor, one long antique table bearing a
bowl of spring flowers its sole furnishing.

She swallowed. His home, she thought. His
London house. And herself delivered there—gift-
wrapped.

She realised suddenly the enormity of what she
was doing.

She could say there'd been a mistake, she
thought wildly. Say she felt ill. Escape now—
while there was still time.

Then the double doors on one side of the hall
swung open, and Rohan stood there, and she
knew that all thoughts—all hopes of escape were

much, much too late.

For a moment, they stood looking at each other, and Cass saw his eyes narrow as if he recognised in her that deep, sudden terror. Then he crossed to her side, smiling easily, lifting both her hands to his lips in a swift, casual caress.

He said softly so that only she could hear, 'Don't run out on me, Cassie. Mrs Grayson is a superb cook, and I don't want her upset, or she might leave.'

She was surprised into laughter, and on that note allowed herself to be led across the hall, and into the room he'd just come from. She looked around at book-lined walls, saw two big, hide sofas flanking an open fire, and felt her heels sink into the softness of a rich Turkey carpet.

She went to the fireplace and stretched out her hands to the flames, but nothing could dispel the chill of apprehension inside her.

'Sherry, darling?' he asked, adding on a note of faint mockery, 'Or would you prefer something stronger?'

'Sherry, please. Dry.' She was thankful to hear how normal her voice sounded. She'd been terrified that she might utter some half-paralysed squeak.

He brought her drink, and took up a position on the other side of the fireplace, resting a relaxed arm on the mantelpiece. Cass looked at the floor, the gleaming fire irons, the sherry like a pale topaz in her glass—anywhere but at him. She'd already seen too much. No dinner jacket tonight, but the most formal of dark suits, elegantly tailored to his lean muscular body, the waistcoat fitting like a second skin.

But what had she expected, she asked in self-derision? That he'd greet her in a silk dressing gown, like some wolf from a Thirties comedy?

He said, 'You look very beautiful, Cassie. But so I'm sure did Anne Boleyn on her way to execution.'

The irony in his tone wasn't lost her, and she looked up flushing.

She said with a little gasp. 'I'm sorry—I shouldn't have come here . . .'

He shrugged. 'Why not? You need to eat, and Mrs Grayson's cooking is worth coming across London for, I promise. And when the meal is over, and we've drunk our coffee, if you're still of the same mind as you are now, I'll get Parsons to drive you quietly and virtuously back to your flat.'

She looked at him blankly. 'Don't you want me to stay?' The words were out before she could stop them.

'Of course.' His mouth twisted slightly. 'But I don't regard it as obligatory either. I hope that reassures you.'

She'd never felt in greater need of assurance. She decided to change the subject. 'You have—another beautiful home.'

'I'm glad you approve,' he said lazily. 'But this isn't wholly mine, and neither is Graystocks. They're family houses which I share with my parents. They're enjoying a very leisurely cruise aboard a friend's yacht at the moment, or you'd have met them at the party.'

She smiled faintly, 'That's probably just as well.'

'Why?'

She shrugged. 'Lloyd was planning to introduce me to his family, but by degrees. Myself first, Jodie much later. I don't think his mother feels a widow with a child is what she has planned for her only son.'

'How very blind of her,' he drawled. 'She should thank God that at least he's had the wit to choose a girl with the ambition and intelligence that he lacks.'

Cass flushed. 'That's not fair.'

'But true,' he said drily. 'What does the woman want? The usual white Anglo Saxon virgin, I suppose, with her brains in her apron.' He smiled at her. 'She should have waited to meet you, Cassie. For a woman who's been married and had a child, you have an intensely virginal quality, as I'm sure Lloyd is aware.'

Her throat muscles contracted. She said, 'Please—don't talk like that.'

'As you wish,' he said pleasantly. 'Drink your sherry, Cassie.' He paused. 'Mrs Grayson will be announcing dinner very soon, and then your ordeal will be nearly over.'

Her flush deepened, and she murmured something incoherent. She was certain that when the time came she wouldn't be able to eat anything. But when eventually she found herself in a small, narrow dining room, its walls panelled in watered silk, with Mrs Grayson placing a plate of fragrant clear soup in front of her, she discovered that her appetite had miraculously revived.

Nor had Rohan exaggerated Mrs Grayson's capabilities. The delicate mousseline of sole which followed was first class, and the noisettes of lamb in a wine sauce almost defied description.

It was probably the most delicious meal Cass had ever eaten in her life, she admitted to herself as she savoured the last few crumbs of the piquant lemon cheesecake which had completed it.

She put her fork down with a sigh. 'That was wonderful.'

'I'll tell Maggie you said so. She'll be delighted.' He paused. 'She'll probably take our coffee back to the library, but if you'd prefer to drink it here with the width of this solid table safely between us, then it can be arranged.'

She didn't look at him. 'It—it doesn't matter.'

But it did matter, and she knew it. All during that marvellous, leisurely meal, Rohan had been making love to her. He hadn't touched her in any way, but then he hadn't had to. The tone of his voice when he spoke, the way his eyes lingered on her each time he looked at her was enough, charging every moment they'd spent together with sensual significance.

The food, the wine, the intimately candlelit room—they were all part of the same gently insidious seduction, and she knew it.

She'd even secretly welcomed it, because it removed the onus of choice from her. But now Rohan had put the game back in her court again.

She walked quietly to the library at his side, still not touching. Apart from his initial greeting, and the moment when he'd passed her the sherry, he had not laid a finger on her, and his restraint bewildered her.

'Will there be anything else, sir?' Mrs Grayson hovered like a benevolent but overweight fairy. 'No? In that case, I'll say good night.'

'Sleep well, genius.' Rohan took a cheroot from

a box on the big desk in the corner, and lit it. 'Oh, Maggie—you might ring the garage for me and tell Parsons he won't be needed again. I'll drive Mrs Linton home myself.'

'Certainly,' Mrs Grayson beamed. 'Good night, sir, Good night, madam.'

Cass's mouth felt dry. 'Good night,' she managed.

'Brandy?' Rohan asked when they were alone.

She shook her head. 'No thank you.'

Although she could certainly do with it, she thought desperately. He must have read her thoughts, and having deciphered the chaos of emotional confusion inside her, decided to reduce the options open to her still further.

She drank her coffee, then poured herself another cup from the big silver pot in front of her. She could feel her spine stiffening in tension with every second that passed. Could feel herself growing more hideously self-conscious.

She forced some more coffee down her tightening throat, and watched him under her lashes, lounging on the sofa opposite, as if he had nothing on his mind except the brandy in the goblet he was holding, and the cheroot he was smoking.

She'd never seen him smoke before, she thought, and swallowed painfully as a sly voice in her head reminded her of all the other discoveries she might be called on to make before the night was over.

Hurriedly, she switched her mind back to his smoking. Perhaps he was nervous too, she thought, then lashed herself with self-derision. The situation, after all, was hardly a novelty to him.

No, he was biding his time, that was all. He was hardly likely to make any serious advances to her while Mrs Grayson could still be heard, moving between the dining room and the domestic quarters, and they could still be interrupted. And Mrs Grayson seemed to be extremely thorough in her clearing up, taking hours over it . . .

Yet there was no need for her to sit here like a dummy. All she had to do was walk to the door, open it, and ask for her wrap. Rohan might not be pleased, but he would hardly utter any protest in front of his housekeeper. And he'd said that he would drive her home, she argued with herself. But did not move.

Eventually, the house went quiet. Somewhere in its depths a door closed with a note of utter finality. Cass could hear nothing but the sigh of the logs on the hearth, and her own hurried breathing.

'I think "Alone at last" is the favoured cliché in this situation,' Rohan said silkily. 'Have you come to any decision yet, Cassie?'

She couldn't speak. She couldn't even look at him. She just shook her head, gripping the fragile handle of the cup as if it was a lifeline.

He tossed the stub of his cheroot into the fire. 'Then I'll make it for you,' he said almost grimly. Two strides brought him to her. He put his hands under her arms, and lifted her to her feet, coolly detaching the cup from her fingers as he did so. Then he slid one arm under her knees, lifting her completely into his arms as if she was a featherweight, and walked with her to the door. He carried her across the hall to the stairs, taking them two at a time, turning the broad, curving bend where the shadows waited . . .

Cass turned her head, burying her face in his shoulder, and her arms slid slowly up around his neck.

At the top of the stairs, he paused, and kissed her mouth, very slowly, and very thoroughly. She was flushed and breathless by the time he took his lips from hers, and carried her along the broad landing, shouldering his way into the room at the end.

Where he set her on her feet.

It was a large room, furnished with stark simplicity in shades of cream and ivory, the deep crimson cover on the huge bed the one vibrant statement of colour, heightened by the illumination from the one enormous shaded lamp which stood by the bed.

The dress fastened with a long sash, and deftly, unhurriedly, he untied it, and unwound it from her slim waist. When it was totally loose, the jade dress fell open, and instinctively her hands came up to cover her bare breasts. His fingers captured her wrists, gently but firmly removing the concealment.

He said huskily, 'Don't hide from me, darling. You can't be ashamed of your body. You're too beautiful.'

The dress was pushed from her shoulders, and fell in a heap at her feet. In a whisper of silk, the long waist slip followed, leaving her naked except for her tiny, lacy briefs.

His voice was soft. 'You put my dreams to shame, Cassie.'

He began to touch her slowly, exploring her

with his fingertips. She gasped silently as the long, stroking caress slid down the vulnerable length of her spine, then forward, tantalisingly, over the swell of her hips, then upwards, over the soft inner flesh of her arms to her breasts. He cupped them gently, sliding his thumbs over the taut excitement of her nipples, sending white-hot shafts of pure sensation to pierce her body and make her whimper in response.

Rohan drew a sharp breath, then lowered his head, kissing the softly swollen mounds with warm, sensuous lips, circling the rigid peaks with his tongue, making her whole being quiver in endless convulsions of pleasure.

She was shaking so much, she had to cling to his shoulders for support. When at last he lifted his head, she collapsed against him, trembling. His hand tangled in her hair, tipping her head back, so that he could look at her face, her fever-bright eyes.

He sounded shaken. 'Darling, I didn't realise . . .' He paused, his own breathing ragged. 'Has there been no-one else, Cassie—in all this long time?'

'No-one.' A stranger's voice, harsh and strained. No-one, she thought. Like this. No-one—ever.

The body she had washed and clothed and tried to ignore seemed to belong to her no longer. The feelings, the sensations now being engendered within her were totally alien—frightening in their implications.

Rohan lifted her gently and put her on the bed. He began to pull his clothes off, his eyes exploring her in restless, passionate desire as he stripped. She turned her head away, biting her lip.

'Shy, darling?' His voice was quiet, his naked body lithe and warm against hers, as he drew her back into his arms. 'There's no need, I swear it. I only want to make you happy.' He parted her mouth with his, kissing her deeply and hungrily, and she responded helplessly, shivering with delight as the long hands slid inexorably down her body, removing her last fragile covering. For a moment she tensed in shock as she felt him part her thighs.

'Hush, love,' he whispered against her lips, as if she had spoken, and his fingers began to move on her, slowly and with silky warmth, creating the start of a rhythm she had never dreamed existed until that moment.

Her body relaxed blindly, trustingly. The seeking hands, the potent heat of his mouth on her eager breasts were luring her, beckoning her to a dimension of pleasure totally outside her experience. She felt a little sob of disbelief rise in her throat. She couldn't comprehend what was happening to her. The magic of this new and startling intimacy was too strong, too powerful.

She lifted her hands and began to touch him in turn, running her fingers over the muscled sweep of his shoulders, down the long line of his back with sweet, frantic urgency. And as if in silent response to this, the sensuous beguilement of his own caress deepened in a stark demand which made her moan, and arch her slim hips against him in involuntary longing.

She was at the edge of the mystery which had eluded her for so long.

She felt him move. Was aware of him no longer at her side, but above her—over her.

Heard him whisper, 'Cassandra.'

She screamed, a high terrified sound, and jack-knifed away from him, her body curling protectively into the foetal position, her hands lifting to guard her face and head.

She said on a little wailing note, 'Don't hurt me—please, don't hurt me. I'll do what you want—anything you want, but don't hurt me.'

'Darling—what is it? What's wrong?'

Hands on her shoulders, turning her, forcing her . . . She shuddered in agony, trying to twist away. 'I know what you like—what you want me to do.' Her voice was high and breathless like a little girl's. 'And I'll do it, I promise I will, if you'll just be kind to me.'

She sat up, her eyes blind, unrecognising, as she pushed him back on the pillows, and bent over him, her shoulders hunched submissively as her trembling mouth sought him.

His fingers bit into her arms as he dragged her upright—shook her.

He said furiously, 'Will you tell me what the hell you're talking about—and what the hell you think you're doing, as well?' The hazel eyes blazed down into hers. 'I want to make love with you, Cassie, not have you—service me as if I was some client in a sleazy massage parlour.'

She looked at him with blank incredulity, then her whole body crumpled, and she began to cry, her body quivering under the force of the long, shattering sobs.

His arms en-folded her, drawing her tightly against him, pressing her wet face into the curve of his neck and shoulder, his hand stroking her tumbled hair, as he murmured soothingly to her.

As the fierce terrible weeping began to subside, he lifted her, putting her into the bed, and drawing the covers over her. She lay quietly, her hands covering her face, her body shaken by an occasional lingering spasm of frightened grief.

His hand touched her shoulder. He said quietly, 'Put this on, Cassie.'

She looked up. He was standing beside the bed, wearing a robe, and holding out what seemed to be a pyjama jacket in heavy black silk.

Cass sat up slowly, clutching the sheet to her. Mouth compressed he helped her put the concealing garment on, his fingers coolly impersonal as he fastened it.

He said, 'Now stay quietly where you are. I'm going to get some brandy.' She began to protest, and he put a silencing finger on her lips. 'I think you need some,' he said, adding wrily. 'And I know I do.'

He was only gone a very few minutes. He gave her the brandy, then lay down beside her outside the covers, putting his arm round her shoulders. She flinched, but his light clasp did not relax.

'You'll have to take my word for it, Cassie, that I've never felt less like sex in my life. You have nothing else to fear from me.' There was a silence, then he said. 'So—who was he?'

'I don't know what you mean.' She swallowed some brandy.

He sighed. 'Yes, you do, Cassie. I want the name of the man who turned the act of love into an act of terror for you.' He paused grimly. 'Was it your husband?'

She said bleakly, 'Yes, it was Brett.'

'Tell me about it.' He shifted slightly, drawing her closer, so that her head was pillowed on his shoulder. 'When did it start?'

She took another sip of brandy. She'd never cared for it, but she could feel it spreading warmingly through her chilled body. She said dully, 'Almost from the beginning. The first time he hit me was on our honeymoon. We were staying in a caravan on a camp site, and I'd forgotten to bring back the lager he wanted from the camp shop. He—slapped me.' She bit her lip. 'I was so surprised I fell over—and he practically grovelled. He—he thought he'd knocked me down. He seemed so horrified, so disgusted with himself that I—I thought it was just a momentary lapse—because he'd lost his temper.'

'But it wasn't?'

'No,' Cass admitted wretchedly. 'In fact, Brett—didn't lose his temper very much at all. That was made it so awful, because I could never see the—danger signs, and—pacify him.'

He said, 'Why in hell didn't you leave him? Go back to your parents and tell them what was going on?'

'My parents died when I was quite small,' she said. 'An aunt brought me up, but we were never close. I did try and tell her once, but all she said was that most men didn't know their own strength, and that I must have provoked him. I was expecting Jodie and she said it had probably made me difficult to live with.'

'Dear God,' he said softly. 'Did he actually hit you while you were carrying his child?'

She nodded. 'He hated me being pregnant. He said I looked obscene.'

'The only obscenity in all this is himself. Why did you stay with him?'

She said bitterly, 'Because like a lot of other women with young babies, I had nowhere else to go. I was eighteen when I was married. I hadn't trained for anything. Everything I've done with my life, I achieved—after Brett died.' She paused. 'I did try to save some money out of the housekeeping, but it wasn't easy.' She looked round the bedroom, at its discreetly understated luxury. 'You've never been poor, and you're not a woman, so you can't know what it was like. You'd never understand.' She stared down at her hands. 'But when Jodie came—it was bearable. He was better after she was born. But he didn't want any more children, he said, so he stopped sleeping with me. He said it was no hardship, because I was frigid and useless.'

'When did he come to that conclusion?'

'From the first, really.' She drank some more brandy. 'He complained because I wasn't experienced—because I didn't know enough. He used to bring books home, and want me to do the things that were in them, and when I didn't want to—he hit me.' She was silent for a long moment. 'Eventually, I think that he had to hit me. That it was the only stimulus that worked for him.'

His hand cupped her chin, turning her to face him. 'But it wasn't like that with us, Cassie. So what made you think . . .?'

'Because you called me—Cassandra.' She said it with difficulty. 'Brett always used to call me that—before—before he . . .'

He said with a great weariness, 'Dear Christ.' There was a brief silence, then he said, 'And Jodie. What started the nightmares for her? You told me once that she'd seen the accident which killed her father.'

Cass swallowed convulsively. 'He began to hurt her too, after a while,' she said. 'I suspected it, but I could never prove it, or make him admit it. He used to laugh at me. But she'd begun to avoid him, and once I heard her cry, and went into the sitting room, and he was just moving away from her. There was a mark on her face.' She shuddered. 'I couldn't stand any more. I just— grabbed her and ran. I had nothing except her, not even my bag. I had nowhere to go, except that I'd read in the local paper that one of those women's refuges had opened in the neighbour-hood, and I had some vague idea of finding it.' She took a deep breath. 'I—ran, straight across the road with Jodie in my arms, and Brett was right behind us. For once, he really was angry. I don't think he'd ever really believed I would leave. And he wasn't looking. There was a lorry. It couldn't stop. I heard the brakes. I turned round, and—we saw it happen.' She stopped abruptly, gagging slightly as the horror rushed over her once more.

'Everyone was very kind,' she said at last. 'The Coroner told me it would have been over at once. That—oh God—that Brett would have felt no pain.' She began to laugh. 'He—he thought I'd be glad to know that.'

His voice was compassionate. 'Hush, darling, hush,' and he held her, pressing her face into his shoulder, until she'd regained her self-contriol.

At last he said, 'And, of course, you said once I reminded you of him. I'm beginning to see now why you reacted as you did when you ran into me that day at Finiston Webber.' He gave a short laugh. 'I misread the signals completely. I was attracted, so you had to be as well, and I told myself the antagonism I sensed from you was simply liberated female contrariness. That I could be a living reminder of your personal nightmare never even occurred to me.'

Cassie shook her head. 'Why should it?' She sank her teeth into her bottom lip. 'I'm sorry,' she said stiltedly. 'I've—ruined everything. Will you take me home, please.'

'To that empty flat?' he asked. 'I don't think that's a very good idea. There are plenty of guest rooms here.' He paused, then said flatly, 'And you have nothing to worry about from me, Cassie, I swear it. I won't come anywhere near you.'

'Thank you.' She didn't look at him. She was tensing against the sudden, unexpected pain which had lanced through her at his words. 'But I'd really rather go home.'

'Then you shall.' The sheltering arm was removed, and with it, to her dazed mind, went all the comfort the world had ever offered.

He picked up her clothes from the floor, and put them on the end of the bed, then bent to retrieve his own clothing.

He said courteously, 'Can you manage? I'll dress in the bathroom but I'll be within call if you need anything.'

Her voice shook slightly, 'I'll be all right.'

He nodded, and left her alone. Cass moved

slowly and reluctantly forcing her trembling limbs to acquiescence, huddling into her garments.

As she retied the sash of the jade dress, she caught a glimpse of herself in the mirror and shuddered. What right had she had to wear such a thing? It was a sexy provocative disguise, but totally fraudulent. Because, underneath, she was still as much an emotional cripple as ever.

The mental numbness which assailed her was beginning to wear off, and shame was taking its place. For the first time in this new life she'd made for herself with such single-minded determination, she'd lifted the curtain on the past for someone else.

No one, apart from the women at the refuge in those first exhausted days knew the truth about her relationship with Brett.

And now, she'd blurted out the sordid details to Rohan Grant, of all people in the world.

She'd made, in fact, an abject, humiliating fool of herself.

Because, as he'd made clear from the first, all Rohan wanted from her was sex. Well, she'd failed him there, and if that wasn't bad enough, had added a complete run-down on her hangups.

The blue-green eyes were wide and bitter, like bruises in the pallor of her face.

No wonder, he couldn't wait to get her out of his bed—out of his life. He'd been kind to her about it all, but behind the sympathy, he must have been embarrassed to death. He'd wanted a sexual partner, a willing woman—not to be burdened by her past emotional traumas.

And she'd led him on. Instead of keeping him

at arm's length, as she should have done, as sanity had suggested she should do, she'd led him on by coming here tonight—by wearing this dress.

He must feel totally defrauded.

By the time Rohan returned, she had herself well in hand, even managing a cool smile in response to his look of enquiry.

In next to no time, it seemed, they were in the car, and driving back through the late night traffic. Rohan was concentrating rather too obviously on his driving. Cass stared rigidly through the windscreen. Neither spoke.

When they reached their destination, he said briefly, 'I'll come up with you,' and switched off the engine.

'There's really no need,' she said stiffly.

'There's every need.' His voice was brusque.

He fitted the key in the lock for her, opened the door, and went ahead of her to put on the lights, checking that all was well.

She followed him mutinously into the sitting room. Rohan dropped the key into her silently outstretched palm.

'Good night, Cassie,' he said quietly.

She took a breath. 'Not good night—goodbye,' she said flatly. 'I don't want to see you again, Rohan.' She swallowed. 'This evening was a terrible mistake—a disaster from every point of view. It was wrong of me to try and—use you, as I did, and I can only apologise.' She paused. 'All I can promise is to stay out of your life in future, and hope you'll have the goodness to stay out of mine.'

There was a silence. The hazel eyes looked

coldly into hers. Then he shrugged. 'If that's what you want,' he said. 'Perhaps it might be best.'

The door closed behind him, and Cass was alone.

She sank down on the sofa, staring blankly ahead of her.

So—he'd gone, without a backward glance, or even a word of regret. Well, it was what she'd asked him to do—what she'd expected, but in some twisted way that made it worse, not better.

She'd feared he would not care enough. Now she knew that he hadn't cared at all, and the realisation was a bitter one which haunted her as she lay, looking into the night shadows, and waiting for the glimmer which would herald dawn.

CHAPTER EIGHT

SHE stayed in bed until late the next morning, dozing in a confusion of half dreams, then coming back to the level of consciousness and misery over and over again.

She was fully roused at last by the sound of the front door buzzer, forcefully used. Cass sat bolt upright, pushing the hair out of her eyes, a startled incredulous hope taking life inside her. She pushed back the covers with trembling hands, grabbing for her robe. She looked dreadful, she noticed almost with detachment as she fled past the dressing table mirror, but there was no time for any kind of camouflage.

The buzzer sounded again, as she struggled with the door chain. Then the door swung open, and with a mixture of confusion and disappointment she could not conceal, she found herself confronting Lloyd.

He walked past her into the room, and waited for her to close the door, his whole stance aggressive.

He said without preamble, 'Is he here?'

Her chin went up. 'Precisely whom are you expecting to find?'

'Don't play games with me,' he said belligerently. 'I've heard all about what happened on Friday night after I left—about you going upstairs with Rohan Grant, and coming down ages afterwards, looking as if—as if . . .'

'Yes?' Cass faced him defiantly. 'I should be most interested to hear how I was looking.'

Lloyd glared at her. 'Like the cat who'd had the cream was one description,' he said sulkily.

Cass raised her eyebrows mockingly. 'Goodness, what a cliché. I do hope it wasn't one of the copywriters.'

'It isn't funny,' he gritted.

'No, it damned well isn't,' Cass returned hotly. 'How dare you come here, making these insinuations.'

He said defensively, 'I rang and rang yesterday evening, but there was no reply. Were you with him?'

'Yes,' she said. 'If it's any business of yours. And—no, we did not spend the night together, and he is not here now. Do you want to search the place?'

He said dejectedly, 'I've made you really angry, haven't I? I didn't intend to . . .'

Cass's voice gentled slightly. 'Then perhaps you shouldn't say any more. In fact, it might be better if you went.'

'Yes.' Suddenly, he looked totally deflated. He said, 'Was there ever a chance, or have I spoiled everything by bursting in here like this?' He saw her hesitate and hurried on. 'All right, you don't have to answer that. I think I knew all along. My mother warned me you had bigger fish to fry . . .'

'How kind of her to take such an interest in a total stranger,' Cass said coldly.

'I didn't mean it like that,' he said wretchedly. 'But, Cass—he hasn't got marriage in mind, and you must know it. He could have anyone he wanted, and when he looks for a wife, he'll pick someone in his own income bracket. Someone without a ready made family for him to take on too,' he added.

The words cut at her like knives, but she said calmly, 'Thanks for the good advice, but I'm not in the market for a second husband, and never was.'

'But we can still be friends,' he said, almost pleadingly.

For a cynical moment, Cass wondered whether he might be afraid of losing face at the agency in view of the inevitable gossip, but decided to give him the benefit of the doubt.

She said, 'We've always been friends, Lloyd. I see no reason why that should change.'

It was a relief to close the door behind him. She went into the little kitchen and made herself a mug of strong coffee, then went back into the living room.

Lloyd's words might have hurt, but they'd contained a truth that she had to face. She'd behaved like a fool, a stupid lovesick idiot. She'd built altogether more on this relationship with Rohan than he wanted, or was prepared to give, But, as his hasty departure from her life had proved, the last thing he wanted was for her to have any kind of dependence on him.

She'd been so pathetically sure when she ran to the door, that it was Rohan waiting there. A sob rose in her throat. She must be mad.

She sat for a long time, thinking, while the coffee cooled in the mug. Then she reached for the 'phone.

The first person she rang was Barney Finiston. She said, 'I have some leave left over from last year. Would it be possible for me to take it now? I'd like to take Jodie away over Easter.'

'I don't see why not,' Barney boomed back genially. 'I suppose you're thinking of abroad. It's still a bit chilly for the seaside here.'

She said neutrally, 'I haven't decided yet. But, thanks, Barney. I'll see you in two weeks time.'

He said, 'You're in a hell of a hurry. What about money? You've got holiday pay due . . .'

'We can sort it out when I come back,' she said hurriedly. 'Goodbye, Barney. My love to Sal.'

Her next call was to Graystocks. A woman whom she gathered was the housekeeper, said, in reply to her query, that Mrs Wainwright had taken the children out in the car for a picnic as soon as they'd all returned from church, and was not expected back until that evening.

'Oh,' Cass said blankly, her plans for bringing Jodie back without delay crumbling round her. 'Will you tell her Mrs Linton called, and that I'll 'phone again later.'

'Certainly, madam.'

Cass replaced the receiver, and sat, biting her lip. One day's delay wouldn't make any drastic difference to her plans, she told herself. And she could use the time in practicalities—sorting out the clothes they'd need to take with them, doing any necessary laundry.

She had no wish to go abroad. She wanted some time in peace that was all, to forget this—temporary lapse from the solitary path she'd chosen. Rohan Grant was a weakness, but she could, she would get over him, and go on with her life as if he'd never existed. But she needed to get away for a while, find somewhere private and unfamiliar where she could rebuild the last few weeks in her life, and allow her wounds to heal.

She couldn't run away altogether, as the first cowardly impulse had dictated. To take Jodie—and run, as she'd done once before.

No, she had a life, a career which she wasn't going to jeopardise, just because she'd made an errant fool of herself over a man. A breathing space—that was all she needed. Then life would go on as usual.

Cornwall, she thought. Or Norfolk, perhaps. She fetched the Sunday papers, lying disregarded on the mat, and began to scan the advertisement columns for details of guest houses and cottages to rent.

She kept busy, but all the same the day seemed endless. Towards evening, she went out and had a meal at a local Italian restaurant, doing less than justice to the hearty lasagne she ordered. When she got back to the flat, the 'phone was ringing.

'Cassie?' Marcia's voice. 'Mrs Jeffries said you'd called. Is something wrong?'

'Not a thing,' Cass was amazed to hear how brightly normal she sounded. 'I just wanted to tell you I shall be collecting Jodie tomorrow. I'm planning a little trip for the pair of us.'

'Oh.' There was a silence while Marcia digested this. 'Well, that sounds very nice, although we shall be sorry to lose her so soon. She rode Cannonball all round the paddock yesterday, by the way. I'd have said she was a natural with horses.' Another brief silence. 'Going anywhere special?'

'I haven't quite decided yet.' Cass decided she

sounded almost maniacally cheerful. 'And I'd rather you didn't mention anything to Jodie. I—I want to surprise her.'

'Of course,' Marcia said amiably. 'It shall all remain a deep, dark secret. What train are you catching down here?'

'I thought the eleven-thirty, if that's convenient.'

'That's fine,' Marcia said. 'I'll have you met at the station,' and she rang off before Cass could utter any kind of protest.

Before she left the following morning, Cass popped downstairs to tell Mrs Barrett what she was planning.

'That's really nice, dear.' Mrs Barrett's approval was immediate and unqualified. 'It'll do you the world of good to get some country air. You still look peaky to me, after that dratted 'flu.'

It was good to have that excuse to fall back on, Cass thought, as she sat in the train, watching the scenery fly past with eyes that saw nothing. Her reflection looked back at her from the window, pale and heavy-eyed, the cheekbones strongly emphasised.

There was no-one waiting for her on the platform of the small station which served the environs of Graystocks. Cass walked through the barrier, and stood looking round her, wondering whether she should hire the station taxi.

But even as she hesitated, Rohan's car swept into the small forecourt, and stopped beside her.

He got out, and stood for a moment, looking at her across the roof of the car, his face expressionless.

Cass swallowed. Her heart was hammering,

and she had to repress an instinct to wipe her suddenly clammy palms down her jean-clad thighs.

'We meet again, I'm afraid,' he said coolly. 'Perhaps you could reserve that stricken expression for the privacy of the car. People are beginning to stare. Now, get in.'

She obeyed with open reluctance, and sat, staring unseeingly through the windscreen. He slid into the driving seat beside her.

'Much as I regret to interrupt your trance, the law requires you fasten your seatbelt.' There was a softly jeering note in his voice, which was not lost on her.

Flushing, she fumbled with the buckle, flinching as his hands took over the task with deft impatience.

She said huskily, 'I thought we agreed . . .'

'And I thought it was a private agreement,' he returned flatly, as he started the engine. 'I could hardly refuse Marcia's request that I meet you without long, boring and potentially embarrassing explanations. It seemed easier to do as she asked.'

So there, Cass thought, her flush deepening unhappily.

She said stiltedly, 'Thank you. That was—thoughtful.'

He shrugged. 'I wasn't feeling particularly considerate. I thought I was just being practical.' He shot a look at her. 'You'll be pleased to hear that Jodie is well, very happy, and having a whale of a time. It seems a pity to drag her away when she's so settled.'

'I'm hardly doing that,' Cass said, stung. 'As it happens, I have plans of my own.'

'So I gather,' he said curtly. 'Plans that involve cutting her off from the rest of the world in your exclusive company yet again. Hasn't it ever occurred to you, my dear Cassandra, that Jodie's nightmares could stem from her constant proximity to you, rather than from anything she may or may not remember about her father or the way he died?'

'What the hell do you mean?' Cass demanded, her voice shaking.

'She's a very sensitive child. It would be very easy for her to pick up the vibrations from you when you're uptight because a man's looked at you, or dared to lay a hand on you. After all, your reactions aren't that dissimilar,' he added flatly.

'Quite the psychoanalyst.' If she was pale now, it was with temper. 'If you have any other theories on how I should bring up my child, I'd be glad if you'd keep them to yourself.'

'I'm not interested in your bloody gratitude. I simply think it's time you stopped feeding this neurosis of yours before you do yourself, and your beautiful daughter, some permanent damage.'

She controlled herself with an effort. 'And I think it's time you concentrated on your driving. I'm sure we've missed the Graystocks turning.'

'Yes, we have,' he agreed casually. 'But as we're not going there, it really doesn't matter.'

She said carefully, 'What did you say?'

'I said we weren't going to Graystocks. When Marcia called me last night, and told me you were planning a holiday, it made my own schemes so much simpler. Everyone's going to have some time away—Jodie at Graystocks with Marcia and the boys. And you with me.'

Cass gasped, her face flaming. 'We're doing nothing of the sort. You let me out of this car right now, you bastard.'

'Stop wrestling with the door,' he advised coolly. 'It's locked, just in case you were planning to risk a broken neck.'

She subsided, biting savagely at her lip. She said, 'This is insane. You can't—abduct me like this.'

'You'd think not,' he agreed. 'Yet, I seem to have managed it. Here you are, and here you'll stay.'

'And precisely what do you hope to gain by this—outrage?'

He flicked an amused glance at her. 'Stop sounding like a Victorian maiden. I intend to teach you not to be afraid of me. It's as simple as that.'

'More amateur psychoanalysis?' Her voice lashed him with bitterness. 'Another problem for Doctor Grant's casebook? Another miracle cure?'

'Your word, not mine,' he said. 'I have no such ambition, Cassie. This isn't some noble rehabilitation scheme. The next time we're in bed together, I want to see something other than fear in your eyes. That's all.'

'Sexual therapy?' she flashed. 'Well, I'm sorry. Your—fees are way beyond my means, so can we stop this ridiculous farce here and now?'

He said grimly, 'It's no farce, Cassie. I'm in deadly earnest, and you'd better believe it. You need to learn that not all men are sadists. And that one tragically unlucky experience doesn't have to sour your entire life.'

'My life is not sour,' Cass's eyes were blazing. 'I was fine—perfectly content, until you started forcing yourself on me.'

'Is that what I did?' She saw the firm lips twist. 'Well, this time there'll be no force, Cassie. You have my word on that.'

She said tersely, 'I wouldn't take your word for what day of the week it was. You have no right to treat me like this—to deceive me into going away with you.'

'Perhaps not,' Rohan agreed drily. 'But did I have any real choice? If I'd simply asked you to come away with me, would you have agreed? I don't think so.'

'How right you are. I said I wanted you out of my life, and I meant it. I don't want your damned pity—or your miracle cures either.'

He smiled faintly. 'Don't you? But surely you knew, Cassie, in your heart of hearts, that I wasn't going to be that easy to get rid of? That there's still too much unsaid, and unfinished between us for me to leave you like that.'

She said bitterly, 'Oh, yes. In other words, you want to have sex with me.'

There was a silence, then he said wearily, 'You're really determined to reduce everything to its lowest possible factor, aren't you, Cassie? Yes, I want to make love with you—ultimately. I wouldn't be human if I didn't, but that isn't all of it by any means. I admit I've tried to rush you in the past . . .'

'That's big of you,' she interrupted contemptuously.

'But what I want now,' he went on as if he hadn't heard. 'Is for us to be together for a while, sharing a roof, with no hassle, and no outside distractions.'

'No hassle?' Cassie gave a derisive laugh, her hands clenched tightly together in her lap. 'You say sharing a roof, but what you mean is sharing your bed.'

He sighed. 'There is more than one bedroom, Cassie. Naturally, I'd prefer you to sleep with me, but I don't insist on it.'

'That is, of course, a relief,' Cass said sarcastically. 'But I hope you don't expect me to be grateful.'

He said drily, 'No, darling. I'm not that unrealistic.'

'And don't call me darling,' she snapped.

'As you please,' he said. 'What would you prefer? She-devil?'

She shot him a hostile glance, and relapsed into silence. She had no idea where they were, and no intention of asking either. But she was aware that they were well away from any main road, travelling through narrow lanes where trees, flaunting their springtime greenery arched to form shadowy tunnels, permitting the filtering sunlight to form a delicate tracery on the road. They met little other traffic, and Rohan seemed in no great hurry to reach their eventual destination.

Perhaps he was having second thoughts. Cass found herself praying that he was. In spite of his assurances, the prospect of being alone with him, living in the same house for perhaps several days, was an unutterable torment.

And she was under no illusion as to why she was with him, she told herself stonily. As far as

he was concerned, as he'd admitted, she was—
unfinished business. An irritation which he
needed, physically, to assuage.

And she needed it too. In spite of everything
that had happened, her newly awakened body
ached, pleaded for fulfilment.

Ached for him, Cass acknowledged in bitter
despair. Because she knew that if she gave in to
the pressure of her senses and emotions, she
would regret it forever.

If she'd been a different person, maybe she
could have settled for what he was offering.
Could have been content, for a while, to dwell on
the margin of his life, and accept it philosophically
when it was over.

But for her to give herself, to belong to him,
knowing that there was no real place for her in
his life, or share in his future, would be
intolerable. No sensual satisfaction, however
intense, could ever compensate for the heartbreak
which would inevitably follow.

And there was Jodie to consider too. Jodie,
who was already too fond of Rohan, and
becoming too involved with the family at
Graystocks. Cass could imagine the child's
disappointment and disillusion when it all came
to an end.

She thought drearily, 'I should never have let
it begin.'

She was aware of the car slowing, and realised that
they must have arrived. She bit back a gasp when
she saw the house. It was low and rambling,
white-painted under a thatched roof, with small
dormer windows. And later in the year when the
wisteria over the doorway came into bloom, and

the climbing roses were in flower, it would probably be too beautiful to be true, she thought.

Rohan parked under a lilac tree on the paved forecourt, and opened his door.

He said pleasantly, 'As you can see, we've arrived. Now, you can either walk to the door in the normal way, or you can be carried there, kicking and screaming if need be. There's no one around to hear or care, anyway. The choice is yours.'

He walked round the car, and opened her door. 'Well, which is it to be?'

She said coldly, 'I'll get there unaided. I've not the slightest wish to feel your hands on me again.'

His expression did not alter. 'As you wish.'

She stood watching as he unlocked the boot and took out two cases.

'Sure you've brought enough?' Cass jibed. 'I, of course, have only the clothes I stand up in.'

'One of these is for you,' he said. 'Mostly Marcia's things, I'm afraid, as we didn't have much time, but she thinks you're roughly the same size.'

'Thank you,' she said. 'And I shall never forgive your sister for her part in this either.'

'She'd be sorry to hear that.' He carried the cases to the front door. 'She likes you.'

'Then she has the oddest way of showing it,' Cass said savagely, following him into the house.

The hall was small and square with a flagged floor, the air redolent of old fashioned polish and pot pourri.

'I'll take the cases up when you've had a look round and decided what room you'll be using,' Rohan said levelly. 'But that can wait until after lunch, I expect you're hungry.'

'Not particularly,' denied Cass, who was starving.

'What a pity.' He smiled faintly. 'Mrs Barber who looks after the place in my absence promised to leave one of her meat and potato pies as a welcome gift. But I'm sure I can manage your share as well.'

He led the way into the sitting room, and Cass, recognising that the wind had been taken out of her sails, followed. It was a big, sunny room, traditionally furnished, with a huge sofa, and deeply cushioned armchairs upholstered in chintz. Paper and kindling was waiting in the big dog grate on the wide hearth, and a basket of logs stood to hand.

'I'll get this going.' Rohan took a box of matches from the mantelpiece. 'The kitchen's the far door on the opposite side of the hall. Perhaps you'd like to make some coffee.'

'Well, I wouldn't.' Cass said ungraciously. 'I'm not here to sleep with you, and I'm not here to cook either. Make your own coffee, if you want it.'

He shrugged. 'It's no real hardship, if that's what you thought. I happen to like cooking, and I only get a chance to practise when I'm down here.'

'And I'm not interested in your domestic arrangements either.' Cass bit her lip. 'All I want to know is when you're going to admit that this whole situation is a mistake, and let me go.'

He added some logs to the fire, now burning up merrily, and stood, dusting off his hands.

He said quietly, 'You're free to leave at any time, Cassie.' He walked over to a Queen Anne bureau in the corner and opened a drawer, extracting a small white card.

He held it out to her. 'The name and telephone number of the local taxi-driver,' he told her. 'You can call him any time you want to, and he'll drive you anywhere you wish to go, and send the bill to me. There's a 'phone on the table behind the sofa, and another on the wall in the kitchen. Now, I'm going to get some lunch. You're welcome to join me, if you want to.'

He walked out of the room, and closed the door behind him.

Moving stiffly, the card clutched in her hand, Cass moved to the telephone. She lifted the receiver and held it to her ear. Held it until the dull purr of the dialling tone seemed to fill the world.

Then, slowly, as if her body was acting independently of her will, she replaced the 'phone on the rest, and pushed the card into the pocket of her jeans.

She would telephone later, she told herself. After lunch. When she could think straight again.

She looked round the bright and beckoning room. Felt its serenity settle on her like a warm coat.

This house—this whole situation spelled danger.

Aloud, she said, like a vow, 'I must get away. I must . . .'

CHAPTER NINE

IN spite of her protest, Cass found she did full justice to her share of the meat and potato pie. The cottage had its own small, elegant dining room, but they ate in the kitchen, sitting at the scrubbed pine table. In spite of its gleaming units, and range of gadgets, the room had a warm, welcoming atmosphere, and as soon as the meal was over, Cass hastily escaped to the back garden.

She felt mean about not offering to lend a hand with the dishes, but she had to stick to her guns—make it clear that there were going to be no concessions. For her own peace of mind, she had to stay aloof, refuse to come even a third of the way to meet him.

The land at the back of the house wasn't nearly as controlled as the pretty rose garden which fronted it. In fact, it was pretty overgrown, although not disastrously so, and Cass could see that someone had already made a start on cutting back the tangle of grass, bushes and undergrowth. Probably the male equivalent of the unknown Mrs Barber, she thought, and turned to go back to the house. She stopped with a start, as she realised Rohan was lounging in the doorway watching her.

She sought for a safely neutral remark. 'This is a delightful place,' she said at last. 'Another family home?'

'No, this belongs to me alone.' He smiled faintly. 'Everyone needs a retreat, Cassie, and this is mine. I found it, bought it, renovated it and now I'm beginning to enjoy it.' He glanced round. 'But this garden's a bit of a problem, because I can't spare as much time to be here as I'd like.'

'You do the gardening yourself?' she asked, frankly surprised.

His smile widened into a grin. 'Did you think cooking was my only accomplishment?' he inquired. 'No, this is my own small wilderness, which I intend to tame—in time.' His eyes touched her mouth like a sudden caress. 'You'll find I can have infinite patience—when I need it.'

'I'm sure you can,' she said huskily. 'But in my case, it won't be necessary, because I'm 'phoning for that taxi right away.'

She'd expected some protest, but he merely shrugged. 'Just as you wish. I'm going to start on those nettles.'

She almost flew into the kitchen and dialled. At first the line was engaged, but when she tried again, a woman's voice answered.

'He's not here, I'm afraid,' she said in response to Cass's query. 'He's taken a gentleman to Brighton, and bringing him back tomorrow sometime.'

'Oh.' Cass's heart sank. 'Well—I'll try again— perhaps tomorrow evening?'

'That might be best,' the woman agreed.

Cass put the 'phone down and looked at it blankly. Tomorrow, she thought. A whole day— and a night—to get through before she could escape.

She wandered restlessly from room to room, catching frequent glimpses from the windows of Rohan working in the garden, scything down weeds with easy competence. Once or twice he paused in his task, and glanced towards the house, and Cass shrank back hurriedly behind the shelter of the curtains, terrified that he might have seen her peeping at him—like some adolescent with a crush, she thought bitterly.

Eventually, she made herself some tea, and after a short inner struggle took him a cup. She'd expected some edged remark about capitulation—and to be interrogated as to why she was still around—but all she got was a casual word of thanks as he took the cup from her.

He'd discarded his shirt, hanging it over the branch of a tree, and his bronzed skin was filmed with sweat. Her eyes were wrenched to him, to the width of his shoulders, the faint shadowing of hair across his chest, and the way it grew in a vee down his flat stomach, the tautness of his ribcage, the way the muscles under his skin rippled as he moved. The breath caught clumsily in her throat as she remembered all too potently the scent of his skin, the play of those muscles under her shyly exploring hands. Remembered what it had been like to be held close in his arms ...

With a start, she realised he was watching her, the hazel eyes quizzical. Oh God, she was practically devouring him with her gaze, and he had to be aware of it. Burning all over, she beat a hasty retreat back to the house.

She could not afford to give herself away like that, she thought desperately. At the moment, he seemed prepared to stay aloof as he'd promised, but she wasn't stupid enough to think that he'd let this situation continue indefinitely. He was playing a cat and mouse game with her, that was all, and she could only hope she would be able to get away from the cottage before he tired of playing games, and made his move. Or, at least, that she would have the strength to resist him.

She was watching without interest some old film on the television set in the sitting room, when he came in.

'That's enough for today,' he said. 'I'm now going to have a bath before I start on dinner.'

'Fascinating,' she said coolly. 'I hope you don't want me to wash your back.'

'Actually, it was more in the nature of a warning,' he said drily. 'At the moment, the cottage has only one bathroom, and there's no lock on the door. I didn't want you to walk in on me by mistake, and think it was some elaborate trap.'

He vanished, leaving her to digest what he'd said. She stayed where she was until she knew he was downstairs again. She could hear the clatter of implements from the kitchen, and sniff various delectable odours beginning to drift through the house. She bit her lip in bewilderment. The man who'd spent the afternoon gardening, and was now cooking dinner for them both seemed to bear no relation at all to the brilliant, unpredictable head of a vast company who'd stormed his way into her life a few weeks earlier. Rohan Grant snapped his fingers and a hundred people jumped.

Had Serena Vance ever seen him like this? she wondered painfully, barefoot, in old, faded denims, and an equally ancient shirt open almost to the waist. Totally relaxed, she thought forlornly, while she, on the other hand, felt as if she was being operated by wires.

At last she ventured upstairs herself. She'd chosen the smallest of the three bedrooms, and he'd made no comment at all.

She would have a bath, she thought, and see if the water could get rid of some of her tensions. But she wouldn't change her clothes. She'd looked through the case which Marcia had provided, and seen the glamorous velvety caftans, clearly intended for intimate evenings at the fireside—something she needed to avoid at all costs. Her own nondescript jeans, and bloused top were a much safer bet.

When she entered the kitchen some twenty minutes later, he was standing at the stove, grilling steaks.

'It's almost ready,' he said. 'Would it be too much like domestic slavery to ask you to toss the salad?'

Silently, Cass complied, watching him serve the steaks on to platters and stow them in the warming oven.

'Soup first.' He brought two fragrantly steaming bowls to the table.

After the first spoonful, she said almost wonderingly, 'You really can cook.'

'Yes.' He sent her a mocking grin. 'Did you think it was just a line?'

She shrugged. 'It just seems—out of character. I mean—you have all these hordes of people working for you.'

'Yes,' he said. 'And I expect good service from them too. But I also believe in self-sufficiency,

Cassie. Being able to cope if necessary in any situation. I thought it was something we had in common.'

'Perhaps,' she said.'But it's a game for you, whereas it's been a necessity for me.'

It was his turn to shrug. 'There's a bad recession going on. Other companies have folded. Maybe Grant's will be next.'

'Do you really think so?' she asked sceptically.

'No,' he said. 'But, if it did, I'd simply start again from scratch. I'd survive.'

She believed him.

She drank the rest of her soup, and watched while he fetched the steaks, and the jacket potatoes which were to accompany them.

'And, of course, Mrs Barber's always lurking in the background,' she remarked as she helped herself to salad. 'Ready to take over when you get tired of this homely bucolic charade.' She smiled tightly. 'Once I've departed, you can go back to being a scourge of industry all over the world. It's a role you're far better suited to,' she added casually. 'I can't think how they're managing without you.'

The hazel eyes glinted. 'Before my father retired, he gave me several pieces of advice,' he said slowly. 'Among them were—never think you're indispensable, and—always make time for your private life.' He paused. 'As he and my mother have been happily married for over forty years, I felt it could be worth following.'

'But presumably his private life was never conducted quite so publicly as yours,' Cass said sweetly. 'Tell me—what does Miss Vance think of this cottage?'

His brows drew together reflectively. 'I think—"Too sweet, darling, and quite terribly quaint" was the general reaction.'

So—she had been there, Cass thought, slicing at her steak with real viciousness. She managed a little laugh. 'Well, traditional British architecture is hardly her kind of thing. Miss Vance's idea of a listed building is probably Tiffany's.' She paused. 'Has she been privileged to see the—domesticated side of your nature?'

Rohan grinned, and offered her a platter of bread, which she refused with a curt shake of the head. 'I can't say she ever showed any interest in my culinary skills.' He sighed. 'But you can't win them all.'

Cass realised she was getting into deep water, and it seemed safer suddenly to make for the shore.

She ate the rest of her meal in silence, declining the fruit and cheese he offered as dessert, asking for coffee alone.

'Why don't you take it along to the sitting room,' Rohan said as he poured it. 'Or will your conscience permit you to sit and watch me struggling to clear up unaided?'

She glared at him as she rose from the table. 'If anyone's conscience is troubling them, then it should be yours,' she said. 'You forced me to come here.'

He gave her a level look. 'I plead guilty,' he said. 'Yet you're still here.'

'Your friend with the taxi is otherwise engaged,' she said.

'My condolences,' he drawled. 'Another few hours of stoical endurance for poor Cassandra.'

She winced. 'Please don't call me that.'

'It's your name, and it's beautiful,' he said quietly. 'And it's time it had pleasant associations for you. Stop locking your skeletons into cupboards. Take them out into the light of day, and see them for what they are—ancient history. The present is what matters, and the future.'

'Yes, sir,' she said rigidly. 'Thank you, sir. Is that the end of today's lecture on homespun philosophy?'

His glance was edged. 'Just be thankful I'm restricting myself to words, darling.'

Curled into a corner of the sofa, her legs tucked under her, nursing her untouched coffee, she tried to be thankful, but it wasn't easy. But it would be over soon, she tried to reassure herself. And when she walked away, her self-respect at least would be intact, if not her heart.

What she must not do was allow Rohan to lull her into a false sense of security. All this gardening, and cooking and keeping at a distance might impose a façade of convention, but they were in an abnormal situation, and she must not forget it.

He'd made no demur when she'd chosen her bedroom, but later, on her way downstairs, she'd passed the open door of his room, and seen the wide double bed which dominated it. In spite of his assurances, he clearly didn't expect to sleep alone when he stayed at the cottage, she thought. His own words, *The next time we're in bed together* haunted her. He believed it would happen. He intended it to happen.

She wished with all her heart that she'd learned to drive. His car was there, under the lilacs, the

perfect means of escape to hand, and totally
beyond her. She could start walking, of course.
But she was by no means certain she could
remember the tortuous route which had brought
them to the cottage, and, besides, how long
would it take him to follow and find her, once
he'd realised she was missing?

She was so lost in her own thoughts, brooding
in the firelight, that she did not hear him coming
along the passage. When the main light was
suddenly switched on at the door, she started
violently, spilling the coffee.

'Oh,' she exclaimed distressfully, getting to her
feet, and mopping at herself with her hand.

He was at her side instantly. 'My God, have
you scalded yourself. I didn't realise you were in
the room. I thought you'd gone up . . .'

She was shaking. 'I'd forgotten the coffee. It
was cold anyway—but the upholstery . . .'

'Damn the upholstery,' he said, passing her an
immaculate handkerchief. 'I'm afraid your clothes
have taken the worst of it.'

She'd already realised that. 'And they're all
I've got to wear.'

His face hardened. 'My sister ransacked her
wardrobe for you,' he said tersely. 'But if wearing
her things is really so impossible, there are
machines in the kitchen which will wash the stuff
you're wearing, and dry it too by morning.'

Cass bit her lip. 'Thank you.'

'Or I could burn them on the bonfire with the
rest of the rubbish,' he went on, as if she hadn't
spoken. 'God knows that's all they deserve. What
in hell do you think, Cassandra? That if you
shroud yourself in ugliness for the rest of your

life, no man's going to take a second glance at you, and you'll be safe?' He gave a short derisive laugh. 'Well, I'm here to tell you you're wrong. Shapeless clothes can be intriguing in themselves. And when a man's seen you—touched you as I have, not even a sack tied over your head's going to cloud *that* particular memory.'

'Please.' She didn't look at him, scrubbing fiercely at her stained jeans. 'Please don't talk like that. Will you show me—how to operate the washing machine?'

He shrugged. 'Leave the things outside your room. I'll attend to them later.' His voice sounded curt, dismissive, and Cass decided it might be safer to be dismissed.

She said, 'Thanks' again, and added a subdued, 'Good night.'

As she hurried back from the bathroom, she could hear the sound of voices from the sitting room, and guessed he had switched on the television, which did not, hopefully, suggest that he had plans for seduction in mind.

She liked to have fresh air while she slept, and she perched on the window seat to deal with the casement, even though she wasn't tired in the least. It was too early, she thought, leaning her forehead against the coolness of the pane, and, besides, she felt too restless, too disturbed to rest.

Her mind kept returning obsessively to the man downstairs. In daylight the situation had been almost bearable. But now that darkness had closed round the cottage, she felt shut in, vulnerable. The night had inescapable connotations, which she didn't want to have to contemplate. Because—if—that door opened, she had no real idea what she would say—how she would react.

The night was cool, and Marcia's pretty voile nightgown was thin, but her body was burning with a pulsing fire she could neither explain nor control. And if Rohan Grant could achieve that effect without one touch, one kiss, what would he do to her if he decided to exert some pressure, she wondered desolately.

All the same, when she heard the door behind her open, she could hardly believe it. She turned slowly and stared at him, her eyes widening endlessly as two strides brought him into the centre of the small room.

She heard the stammer in her voice. 'W-what do you want?'

'Your clothes,' he said enunciating carefully as if she were deaf—or just plain stupid. 'You were supposed to leave them outside for me. Or have you decided to risk wearing some normal gear tomorrow instead?'

Her jeans and top were lying on the bed. All he had to do was reach out a hand and pick them up, but by the time she realised that she was halfway across the room to fetch them—only checking when she saw him watching her, saw the total absorption, the frank sensual appreciation as he studied the cling of the flimsy nightgown to her breasts and thighs as she moved.

Her face was burning as she snatched up the bundle of clothing and held it out to him. 'Here,' she said stormily.

He smiled derisively at her tone, but his hazel gaze was riveted to her mouth.

His hand reached out and closed round one

slim bare arm, drawing towards him not forcibly, but firmly, brooking no resistance.

If she'd been burning before, now the first beguiling warmth of his mouth on hers made her shiver. It had been all eternity since the last time she'd felt his body against hers, known the insidious enchantment of his lips parting hers, the subtle invasion of his tongue . . .

Blindly, she swayed towards him, and felt, incredulously, the grip on her arm tighten as he put her away from him.

'Good night,' he said pleasantly. 'If you need anything in the night, then you know where to find me.'

With incredulity, she watched the door close behind him, then sank down on the edge of the narrow bed as if she'd been poleaxed, burying her fevered face in her hands.

It was late when she woke the following morning, and the sun was streaming into the room through a gap in the pretty sprigged curtains. For a moment she stared around, disorientated, then, remembering, she collapsed back on the pillows with a little groan, resisting an impulse to drag the covers over her head and stay there forever.

She sat up again, very slowly. She'd lain awake for what seemed hours the previous night, listening for Rohan coming to bed. When, at last, she'd heard his footsteps on the stairs, she'd tensed urgently, burrowing down in the bed, wondering crazily whether she could fool him into thinking she was asleep when he came into the room.

Only, he had not come into the room. He'd

walked past. Ears straining frantically in the dark, she'd heard him go into the bathroom, then later the quiet closing of his door. After that, silence.

And while Cass had been trying to figure out whether her predominating emotion was relief or disappointment, she'd fallen asleep.

But she was wide awake now, she thought drily. Wide awake, and worried.

She began to push aside the covers, then paused, as she saw her jeans and top neatly folded, lying on the window-seat. It made her feel vulnerable to know that he'd been in her room while she was asleep. And not for the first time either, she thought, her mind flicking frowningly backwards to that bout of 'flu when she'd half-woken, and seen him there.

She washed and dressed and went downstairs. The aroma of coffee filled the kitchen, and from the window she could see Rohan hard at work in the garden. She poured herself some coffee and walked out into the sunshine, drawing the fragrant air deep into her lungs with instinctive delight.

'Good morning.' Rohan had straightened at her approach, and was watching her, his face cool and speculative. 'Did you sleep well?'

Cass flushed slightly. 'I think you know I did.' She gestured awkwardly at her clothes. 'Thank you for these. You're—very efficient.'

He shrugged. 'You're my guest.'

'I'm your prisoner,' she retorted.

'Any cage you feel around you, Cassandra, is of your own making,' he said levelly. 'I'm not adding any bars—merely trying to remove some that already exist. Set you free, in fact.'

But freedom wasn't the gift she wanted at his hands, she thought achingly.

'So, how are you planning to spend your captivity today?' he asked mockingly as the silence between them lengthened. 'Pacing round the house like a little tigress again? Because you could always lend a hand out here, if it's not against your principles.'

'I don't know anything about gardening,' she protested.

'At this stage there isn't a lot to it,' Rohan said drily. 'Just assume everything you find growing is a weed and behave accordingly.'

Cass lifted an indifferent shoulder. 'Why not? At least it will fill in the hours until I can get out of here.'

'It might,' he said. 'And—who knows? You might even get to enjoy it.'

That was the danger, Cass thought numbly, as she began to obey his directions. Unless she was careful, she could find herself wanting to stay here with him forever.

And there was Jodie, she reminded herself guiltily. Jodie, who didn't know where she was, who might be fretting for her. She'd hardly given her a thought since she arrived here. She tried to assuage her feeling of treachery by reminding herself she could be reunited with her that evening if everything worked out.

In the meantime, she was discovering that the hard manual work of gardening brought a curious satisfaction all its own. There'd been a garden in the house where she was born, but her aunt had lived in a flat with not even a window box, and the house she'd shared with Brett had fronted directly on to the street, with a small yard for hanging washing at the rear.

She was amazed how quickly the time passed. It seemed like minutes before it was lunchtime. They ate a snack meal of paté and french bread, washed down with lager, then started again.

Cass felt a real sense of pride at the size of the patch she'd cleared as she straightened, giving a little gasp as her muscles protested volubly.

Every inch of clothing seemed to be sticking clammily to her body, and her back and shoulders were shrieking for surcease.

Rohan looked across at her, frowning a little.

'You've done enough,' he said. 'Go and soak in a hot tub, while I finish up here.'

It was a command, but she was in no state to resent it. A hot tub, she thought thankfully, as she headed for the house. The greatest idea since the beginning of the world, she decided as she began to run the water into the bath, beating the theory of relativity into a cocked hat.

There was bath oil in one of the cupboards, and she added a generous measure before lowering herself with a sigh of pure pleasure into the steaming, scented foam. She'd folded a small hand-towel and placed it against the rim of the bath as a cushion, and she leaned her head back on it, closing her eyes as the water soothed her tired body.

Rohan said, 'Has no one ever told you falling asleep in the bath can be dangerous? It's just as well I've brought you a stimulant.'

Her eyes flew open, and her lips parted in a startled yelp of sheer shock. She almost sat up, but some sixth sense warned her that her semi-recumbent position offered far better concealment, so she stayed where she was.

He put a mug of coffee down on the broad rim of the tub. He was wearing, her stunned mind registered, nothing but a towel loosely draped round his hips.

He smiled at her. 'I did warn you this was the only bathroom, darling, and you can't expect to hog it forever. You've already had more than your allotted span, so drink your coffee and hop it.' His hands moved almost casually to the towel. 'Unless you'd like me to join you.'

'No,' she said in a strangled voice. 'And get out of here—now.'

His smile widened. 'Or you'll do—what? Speaking as an observer I'd say you were at something of a disadvantage.' His hand scooped up a handful of the remaining foam and blew it at her gently. 'See what I mean?'

'Yes.' She glared at him. 'Give me a few minutes' privacy, and the bathroom's yours.'

'I think I prefer it the way it is,' he told her silkily. He reached into a cupboard, and produced a small bottle. 'Oil,' he said succinctly. 'Well rubbed in, it will take some of your backache away.'

'Thank you,' Cass said hurriedly. 'If you'll just leave it within reach . . .'

He shook his head. 'It needs to be applied now—while you're warm and relaxed. And you certainly can't reach all the relevant spots yourself. So—sit up a little.' He handed her a large sponge. 'You can preserve your modesty with this, if you feel you must, although I should remind you yet again there's nothing the matter with my memory,' he added sardonically.

He was uncapping the bottle, and pouring oil into the palm of his hand.

Slowly and cautiously, using the sponge as a shield, Cass sat up.

For the first few moments, the stroke of his fingers across her taut skin was sheer physical pain, but gradually under the firm rhythmic pressure of his hands, the knots of tension began to dissolve away almost magically, and she began to relax under his touch, even to co-operate, as a little sigh of satisfaction escaped her lips.

He said softly into her ear, 'I told you cooking wasn't my only accomplishment. Bend your head a little.'

She obeyed, quivering with pleasure as he began to massage the nape of her neck, her head moving almost involuntarily in response to the caress of his strong fingers.

His hands slid to her shoulders and paused, and her body arched, leaning back against him, the sponge slipping from her nerveless grasp to reveal the lift of her small breasts, the rosy nipples darkly erect with excitement.

She turned her head into his bare chest, feeling his heartbeat beneath her cheek, hearing the note of his breathing change.

She was waiting. Ah God, she'd been waiting so long it seemed, and he couldn't be so cruel as to string out this fevered anticipation any longer . . .

Slowly, slowly, his hands glided down from her shoulders, making her ache again, but so differently. Aching in an agony of expectation—of sheer desire.

Then, with a suddenness which seemed to drive all the breath from her body, his hands

hooked under her slender armpits, and lifted her
bodily out of the water, setting her firmly on her
feet on the fleecy carpet. And instead of the
longed-for caress, she felt the warm friction of a
bath towel enveloping her.

She looked at him dazedly, aware that her
drowsing eyes, her parted lips were telling him
how totally vulnerable she was, and not caring
any longer.

'I think that's enough for now.' Was that
mockery she could hear in the quiet voice? she
wondered, cringing. 'But if you need further
treatment, you only have to let me know.' His
hands lifted, cupping her face, his fingers tangling
in her dampened hair as he stared down at her.

She thought he was going to kiss her, but he
didn't. Instead, she experienced the blatant sensual
thrust of his lean hips against her softness,
demonstrationg with silent force all the heated
strength of his arousal. And, for a shattering
moment, she felt her own body flare in response so
acute it almost tore a cry from her throat.

His hand tightened in her hair. He said softly,
but with an undertone of menace, 'Perhaps you'd
better get out of here while I'm still prepared to
let you.'

She stumbled to her room, almost tripping
over the trailing towel. Once inside, she slammed
the door, and leaned back against the panels, her
breath labouring in suddenly tortured lungs.

For her own sake, she had to find the strength,
somewhere, to fight him. But time, it seemed,
was running out fast. And so, God help her, was
her will to resist him.

CHAPTER TEN

As darkness fell, Cass was sorely tempted to stay in her room with the door locked. But wasn't that merely another form of self-betrayal, she wondered bitterly.

No, it was better to go downstairs and join him for dinner as if nothing had happened. Which, in truth, it hadn't, so the thing to do was play the whole incident down.

She'd dirtied her jeans and top again during her afternoon's endeavours in the garden, so she was forced to fall back on Marcia's selection after all. But she chose with care, deliberately rejecting the sensuousness of the evening wear for the chic black flare of a soft wool skirt, which she teamed with a full-sleeved cream silk blouse cut on classic lines.

She delayed her arrival downstairs until the last possible moment. The sitting room was empty although the fire crackled softly in the grate, and, after a brief hesitation, she went along to the kitchen.

Attempting to establish an atmosphere of normality, she said, 'The food smells wonderful.'

Rohan who was standing at the stove looked round at her. He was wearing black too, she noticed, her eyes drawn instinctively to the lean contours of his body.

'We aim to please,' he commented sardonically. 'Sit down and pour some wine. You look as if you need it.'

Aware that her colour had heightened, she obeyed, while he brought the food, a chicken casserole and a bowl of savoury rice, to the table.

The unwonted activity in the fresh air had sharpened her appetite almost ravenously, in spite of the emotional turmoil she was in, and she ate every scrap placed in front of her.

'But I don't want any coffee, thanks,' she said, lifting a hand to her mouth to conceal an artificial yawn. 'I—I think I'll have an early night.'

'Not yet,' he said brusquely. 'And if you don't want coffee, you can at least bear me company while I have mine. Go along to the sitting room and wait for me there.'

The autocratic note in his voice infuriated her, and she flung her head back, her lips parted in defiance, then faltered as she read the message in the cool hazel eyes fixed steadily on her own.

'Very wise,' Rohan approved drily after a moment's silence. 'Now, run along.'

Cass stood in the middle of the sitting room, her arms crossed defensively over her body while she stared huntedly round her. The purpose she'd seen in Rohan's face had been unmistakable. He'd interpreted her frenzied reaction to him in the bathroom quite correctly, she thought bitterly, and clearly saw no reason to hold back any longer.

But—she couldn't let it happen. She wouldn't let it happen. She couldn't endure a lifetime of regret for the sake of one night's passion.

The taxi, she thought feverishly. Perhaps the driver was back, and could come to collect her right away. She reached for the 'phone, only to remember the vital number was upstairs in her room. Cass sped to the door and halted as she heard Rohan coming down the passage. Controlling a groan of dismay, she shot to the sofa, and sat down on its edge, smoothing her skirt over her legs with hands that trembled.

As he came in, she regretted choosing the sofa, in case he interpreted that as a mute invitation to come and sit beside her. But instead he went to one of the armchairs and dropped into it, stretching his long legs to the glow of the fire. Then he looked across at her.

'Relax,' he said wearily. 'You look like a cat on hot bricks.'

'Is it any wonder,' Cass retorted. 'Do you think I have no feelings at all?'

'No,' he said. 'On recent evidence, that's the last thing that would occur to me.' Without a change in inflection, he went on, 'Sure you couldn't use some coffee? I promise not to startle you into spilling it this time.'

She gave a constrained smile. 'I dare not risk it—not while I'm wearing your sister's beautiful clothes.'

He leaned back watching her through half-closed eyes. 'Well, there's a simple solution to that particular problem,' he said softly. 'Come over here, and I'll show you.'

Her body went rigid. 'No.'

'Why not?' he asked. 'The room is warm. The cottage is private. No-one's going to walk in on us.'

She ran the tip of her tongue round dry lips. 'Because—because I refuse to be—used as a sex object by you.'

'All right,' Rohan said equably, his mouth

slanting into a smile. 'Then why don't you use me as one instead? I promise you won't hear one word of complaint.'

She said huskily, 'I can't.'

'Then come here.' His voice was implacable. 'Or do I have to fetch you?' He waited for a moment, then rose to his feet and came over to her. He took her wrists and drew her gently but inexorably upright, so that she was facing him. He said gently, 'I want to hold you, darling. I want to kiss you. I want to feel every warm sweet inch of you against me as I did that night in London. And, if you wish, it can stop at that. Only—be close to me now.' His arms went round her, pulling her to him. For a long moment, she stood, wrapped in his embrace, then her body slackened, shaking, against his, and of her own accord she lifted her mouth, blindly, seeking his kiss.

His lips were tender on hers, making few demands, allowing her to set the pace. She began to touch him shyly, running her hands along the strong line of his shoulders, and after a moment he whispered, 'Wait' while he peeled the thin black sweater over his head, and tossed it away. 'Now.' He drew her hands back to him again, holding them against the muscled wall of his chest, the strong beat of his heart.

Her fingertips moved on him slowly, learning him, sensing his pleasure as her caresses became less tentative. He kissed her again, coaxing her lips apart, exploring her mouth intimately, then, without taking his lips from hers, he sank down on to his knees on the big fur rug in front of the fire, taking her with him to kneel before him.

Slowly, as if he had all the time in the world, he began to free the little mother of pearl buttons which fastened her silk shirt. Cass shivered as she felt the soft glide of the material from her shoulders, and down her arms as he removed it. For a moment his fingers teased her, playing almost idly with the scalloped lacey edge of her bra, tracing the soft mounding of her breasts where they swelled from the confining cups. Then the restricting clip snapped open, and his hands cupped her instead.

Her head fell back with a little, helpless sigh of pleasure as he caressed her, his fingers a sweet, inciting torment against the swollen rosy nipples. His mouth slid down to her throat, exploring the soft hollows at its base, then feathering a leisurely path downwards, his tongue curling into the scented cleft between her breasts.

His lips began to verify the excitement he had created, brushing the hard peaks as lightly as a butterfly's wing, making her body arch, shuddering with delight. At the same time, his hands were moving downwards, freeing her from the clinging folds of her skirt. Then, gently, he lowered her so that she was lying on the rug. The long fingers stroked down her body once in promise and anticipation, then he lifted himself away from her. Lying, the firelight flickering on her half-closed eyes, Cass sensed the soft sounds and movements as he undressed—the clink of his belt buckle, the rasp of his zip.

When he took her in his arms again, she turned to him, her whole body an ache of welcome, gasping as the hair-roughened texture of his skin grazed her own from breast to thigh.

His mouth sought her breasts again, hungrily and possessively, using his tongue to pleasure the urgent nipples. His hands slid over her, intimately, sensuously, and everywhere he touched, little coils of intensity began to burn, consuming her.

He whispered raggedly, 'Must I stop, darling. Must I?'

Against the softness of her thighs, she could feel the hardness of him, the potent strength of his maleness demanding access.

She kissed him on the mouth, her tongue flicking restlessly, fiercely against his, her hands sweeping down his body, exploring from his shoulders to the narrow muscular flanks, hearing the breath rasp in his throat as he fought for control.

Her mouth still locked to his, she made the slight, languorous movement of her body which was all that was needed to accommodate him. Felt his own movement in response, the breath catching in her throat as she experienced the gentle sublety of his penetration of her. In this, as in everything, he was unhurried, and when, at last, his possession was total, complete, he wrapped her in his arms, and lay holding her, joined to her, giving her time to savour the intimate wonder of his body in hers.

Then the warm weight of him lifted from her slightly, and he began to move, slowly, easily at first, beckoning her, luring her into some strange and secret world. Caught up in the rhythm he had initiated, she moved with him, responding to sheer instinct as her slim hips arched in answer to his thrusts.

The firelight was turning his bare skin to bronze, she thought, worshipping him with her eyes as he worshipped her with his body. Yet coherent thought was becoming difficult. The focus of her attention was changing, turning in on herself to her innermost physical being, and the new sensations he was creating for her. Need was spiralling—was becoming wild urgency. She couldn't control it any more than she could control the little moans bursting from her taut throat, the fierce supple twisting of her body in reply to his quickening, deepening demands.

He mouth clung, heatedly, hungrily to his. Her fingers bit into his shoulders, her slim legs gripping him with a kind of desperation as she sought for her release.

And when, at last, it came, she was almost overwhelmed. Wave after wave of delight tore through her, convulsing her in spasms so intense she thought she might die. She could hear her voice crying something in frantic disbelief, and his voice groaning an answer as he reached the climax to his own pleasure.

Then the storm passed, leaving her folded in his arms as she had been when it began.

Rohan was the first to stir, levering himself up on one elbow to look down at her, his hand stroking the curve of her passion-flushed face.

'My Cassandra,' he said huskily. 'My wild, sweet angel.'

She smiled at him shyly, then captured his stroking hand and pressed it to her lips. 'Thank you.'

He shook his head, frowning slightly. 'Don't go humble on me, darling. The pleasure was entirely mutual, and you know it.' He pushed the sweat-dampened hair back from her forehead, kissing her temples, her eyes, the tip of her small, straight nose. He murmured 'I can see my nights are going to take on a whole new dimension from now on.' He rolled on to his back, taking her with him, so that she was lying on top of him. 'When I've regained sufficient strength to tackle the stairs, we'll have that early night you mentioned.'

She pantomimed astonishment. 'You mean—again?'

He sent her a lazy grin. 'That was just your starter for ten. Let's see how many bonus points you can earn.'

'When would you like me to start?' She bent her head, and delicately licked his flat nipples.

His brows lifted provocatively. 'Now?' he suggested.

She woke early the next morning and lay for a long time, boneless as a kitten, watching him sleep.

She felt amazing, she thought. Twice as alive as usual, if that was possible. In fact until last night, apart from giving birth to Jodie, she wondered whether she had ever been alive at all.

She stretched luxuriously, but gently, reluctant to disturb him. He deserved his rest, she thought, a mischievous smile curving her mouth. She'd wake him later, as he'd woken her sometime during the night, with kisses . . .

A little shiver of anticipatory desire rippled through her, and she had to bite back a laugh of sheer exuberance.

Apart from teaching her with utter finality that

she was not and never had been frigid, he'd had other lessons for her. She'd never imagined, for instance, that passion could be commingled with laughter, and enhanced by it. Never guessed that someone so strong, so totally masculine could be so gently intuitive to her every need, almost before she was aware of them herself. Never dreamed she could be coaxed into taking the initiative, lured into showing him quite explicitly what she wanted—even into telling him. Whatever lingering inhibitions she might have had, no longer existed.

Cass sat cautiously, sliding back the covers, and shivering a little as the cool morning air met her warm nakedness. His robe was lying across a chair, and she put it on, even though it swamped her. Their clothes were still downstairs, strewn all over the hearthrug, and she felt they should be moved, just in case someone decided to intrude on their privacy after all. She'd make some coffee too, and bring it back to bed, she thought as she went downstairs, holding up the hem of the robe so she didn't trip on it.

It was an odd disappointment, almost a shock, to find that it was raining, the sky thick with threatening cloud. Cass had been expecting the sun-drenched promise of the previous day to match her mood. Before they'd finally fallen asleep, Rohan had murmured something about driving over to Graystocks to see Jodie. The rain wouldn't prevent that, but it would make a difference to their plans for how to spend the day.

She smiled to herself, envisaging Jodie's delight when she saw them, then stopped abruptly in her self-appointed task of retrieving their scattered clothing, huddling the robe further around her to combat a sudden feeling of chill. The glowing joy which wrapped her around was beginning to subside as reality took over. What was it people said about the cold light of day?

She took the clothes upstairs, then trailed down slowly to the kitchen where their percolator was gently bubbling. She poured herself a cup of the brew, black and strong, and carried it over to the table. She would take Rohan's up presently, she thought, but first she had to think.

Because the plain fact was that last night, however world shattering and tumultuous it had been for her, had basically changed nothing. She had been seduced by an expert, but that was all. There was no future in their relationship, and never had been. Rohan had marked her as his prey, stalked her, and caught her. There were no excuses she could make. She'd fought a losing battle from the beginning, and in the end, she'd run out of defences against him.

Now she was in the trap she'd dreaded. Just another name on the list of ladies who'd been invited to share his life and his bed for a while. And when it was over, in however many days, weeks or months that it took, she would be expected to accept the situation with a good grace, and retire back to obscurity, with her memories to sustain her.

She sank her teeth into her lower lip until she could taste blood.

But in her case, there was an extra factor to be taken in account. Her daughter, whose stability and long term security should have been her own prime consideration. Little Jodie, who'd already shown how desperately keen she was to have a father-figure in her life, and demonstrated, embarrassingly, her readiness to place Rohan in that role.

But that could not be, and Cass knew it. And if she allowed her relationship with Rohan to develop any further, Jodie was bound to be involved, to build up hopes, expectations of Rohan that he could not fulfil.

She swallowed convulsively. Young, lonely widows, with young, vulnerable children could not afford to indulge in casual affairs. The happiness they brought was only transient. The heartbreak when they ended, guaranteed. And the effect on Jodie when Rohan backed away from them could well be catastrophic.

She drank some more coffee. Rohan would know that, of course. He was far from insensitive. In fact, it was perfectly possible that he might continue the affair, long after she'd ceased to hold any real attraction for him, out of a sense of obligation, merely because she was not one of the glamorous, sophisticated types like Serena Vance with whom he was usually involved.

But she didn't want him to feel obligated. No man wanted a ready made family foisted on him, as Lloyd had so cruelly pointed out to her. But the cruelty made the observation no less true. The last thing in the world she wanted was for Jodie and herself to become a burden on Rohan, an albatross round his neck. And the torture of waiting for the blow to fall, waiting for the kind of rapture they'd shared together to dwindle into kindness and a sense of duty was too awful to comtemplate.

Pain tore through her, ripping her apart. No, better to end it now, while she was still capable of doing so. Before she made the fatal error of telling him she loved him.

He'd done so much for her, she thought. She had no right to impose the weight of her love and Jodie's need on him. Because of Rohan, she was a woman at last. He'd achieved what he'd set out to do. He'd made her free—free of fear—free of the haunted past.

Now, in return, she could liberate him too. She pressed her knuckles against her quivering lips, suppressing a sob. And now that she knew what she had to do—for everyone's sake—the sooner it was accomplished the better.

The taxi-driver sounded surprised to receive a call so early in the morning, but he agreed he was available, and they fixed a time for him to fetch her.

Moving like a ghost, Cass washed and dressed, using with reluctance some more of the clothes Marcia had provided—a classically cut tweed skirt this time, and a thin russet coloured sweater.

She'd asked the taxi-driver not to come to the door. It was essential that Rohan had his sleep out. If he woke, and discovered what she intended, he might try and weaken her resolve, and she could not afford to let that happen. She felt as if she was dying inside as it was.

While she watched for the car, she found paper and a pen in the bureau, and wrote him a note. It took several attempts before she felt she'd managed the correct blend of casualness and finality.

'Thank you for setting me free,' she wrote. 'And goodbye.' She signed it and propped it on the mantelpiece against the carriage clock where it would be impossible for him to miss it.

There was still no sound from upstairs when she saw the taxi arrive. She tried very hard to feel relieved as she unlocked the door, and shut it silently behind her—relieved that her departure had been, physically, so simple. Emotionally, of course, it was a different matter.

She tried hard to compose her face for the taxi-driver, a grizzled man who came forward to take her case from her, giving her a searching look as he did so.

She wanted him to be able to tell Rohan, if he asked, that the lady had left with a smile, and her head held high, not awash with tears.

If he disregarded the tone of her note, and came in search of her, she would have to think of something that would drive him away, in disgust if necessary. Let him think, perhaps, that what had passed between them had been prompted by mere sexual curiosity on her part. And that, while she was grateful, she had no further curiosity left. She could say it with amused regret, she thought wretchedly. She could even, God help her, let him think she was going to marry Lloyd.

But he wouldn't come after her. Why should he, when he'd had what he wanted from her. He'd put her sudden desertion, cynically, down to experience, and next time choose a woman who'd play the game his way.

She sat in silence, glad that the driver was not a talkative man, while her brain went round wretchedly, over and over again, on the same

tired treadmill, only aroused from her bitter
reverie when the car turned in through the wide
iron gates at Graystocks.

'Shall I get your case,' the driver asked as he
opened her door.

'No, thanks,' Cass said hurriedly. 'Perhaps
you'd wait, and drive me to the station.'

He nodded his agreement, and Cass trod
quickly up the broad, shallow steps which led to
the front door, and rang the bell. The manservant
who answered the door gave her a surprised look
when she asked for Marcia.

'Mrs Wainwright is breakfasting in her room,
madam. I'll take your name and . . .'

'No, please don't disturb her,' Cass broke in.
'I—I've just called to collect my little girl. We
have to get back to London rather urgently. I
have a taxi waiting.'

The man's face relaxed into a smile. 'Miss
Jodie's in the nursery, madam. But I'm sorry to
hear she's leaving us, I'm sure. May I show you
up or . . .'

'I know the way,' Cass assured him.

The first person she encountered in the
nursery wing was Nanny.

'Mrs Linton?' The older woman exclaimed.
'My, but you're an early bird. There's nothing
wrong, I hope.'

'Nothing.' Cass pinned on a smile. 'But I do
need to go home. I have—plans for Easter.
Perhaps you'd pack Jodie's things, or show me
where they are,' she added hastily, seeing Nanny
frown.

'I'll pack for her, of course, madam,' Nanny
said, after a pause. 'But I'm sure Miss Marcia

had no notion of her leaving yet. In fact . . .' she paused again.

Cass bit her lip. 'Miss Marcia has been endlessly kind, but we really mustn't trespass on her hospitality any further,' she said quietly.

Nanny's brows rose, but she made no further comment. She opened a door, and said, 'James—Simon—come with me a moment, my dears. Jodie's Mummy has come, and wants a word with her, I think.'

The boys trooped off obediently, giving Cass shy grins as they passed. The sight of them gave her another pang. The family resemblance was strong in the next generation too. Rohan's sons would probably look much the same . . .

Jodie leapt off from the table and launched herself at her mother. 'Mummy,' she said rapturously. 'What are you doing here? Auntie Marcia said you were having a nice long holiday. Have you come back because it's raining? I wish it would stop, because I want to ride Cannonball. Peter who looks after all the horses says I have really good hands.' She looked past Cass, her brows drawing together. 'Where's Rohan?'

Cass's heart missed a beat. 'Why—do you ask that?' she enquire unevenly.

'Because he was going on holiday with you. He told me so. He said I wasn't to worry, because he'd look after you.'

Cass smiled with a tremendous effort. 'Yes—well, the holiday's over now, darling, and we have to go home.'

Jodie's frown deepened. 'Is Rohan going with us?'

'No, sweetheart.' Cass coaxed Jodie to sit down

beside her on the big, sagging sofa which stood in front of the nursery fireplace. She put an arm round the child's suddenly tense body. 'Jodie, there's something you've got to understand. We have our life, and Rohan has his. We can't—impose on him any more.' She paused, carefully controlling her voice. 'So, I'm afraid we won't be seeing him again.'

There was a terrible silence. When she nerved herself to look at Jodie, the stricken look in the little girl's eyes took her by the throat. The damage, she thought desperately, had already been done, it seemed.

'Darling,' she appealed. 'Try and see things Rohan's way. He's an important man. He has a huge company to run, lots of responsibilities. He's been very kind to both of us, but we can't expect him to go on spending all this time . . .

'But he said. He promised.' Jodie's voice cut across her words, almost cracking with the passion of her distress. 'Before he went away, he told me you were going to marry him, and that he was going to be my real daddy, and that he'd love us both, and look after us forever.'

Agony clenched in Cass. She said, 'Jodie, that's just wishful thinking on your part, and you know it. Did you ask him about being your daddy again, in spite of everything I said to you the first time?'

'No, no I didn't.' The tears were raining down Jodie's face now. 'He told me all about it. He gave me a big kiss, and said I had to wish him luck. He said I could be a—a bridesmaid in a pink dress, and have a puppy, and a swing in his garden, and brothers and sisters.' Her voice rose in a wail of total desolation.

The door opened, and Marcia swept in, hastily tying the ribbons of a silk and lace negligée.

She said sharply, 'Cassie? What the hell's going on here? Why is Jodie in such a state—and where's Rohan?'

'At the cottage. Asleep.' Cass got to her feet. 'I've come to take Jodie home.'

'Did you have to reduce her to hysterics first?' Marcia's tone held censure. She sank down in a froth of scented frills, and drew Jodie into her arms, soothing her gently. 'There, sweetie, there. Don't cry. Rohan will be here in a minute, and he'll make everything better, you'll see . . .'

'But he won't,' Jodie sobbed passionately. 'Mummy says we're never going to see him again.'

Across the top of her head, Marcia's eyes met Cass's in a kind of horrified disbelief. She said half to herself, 'Oh, my God.' Then, raising her voice, she called, 'Nanny dear, are you there?'

Nanny appeared with suspicious promptness, her face a mask of discreet concern.

'Take Miss Jodie, and wash her face,' Marcia said, pulling herself together briskly. 'And I think she might have one of her Easter eggs in advance, don't you. I'll take Mrs Linton downstairs.'

Cass hung back. 'I've a taxi waiting.'

'Then I'll get Jeffries to send him away,' Marcia said brusquely. 'You can't take Jodie anywhere in that state. And besides, you and I have some talking to do,' she added grimly.

'There's nothing to talk about,' Cass said in a low voice. 'Marcia, I suppose you mean to be kind, but you've got to allow me to know best about my own life.'

Marcia, halfway down the main stairs, turned in a swish of silk to confront her. 'Are you saying you actually don't want to marry Rohan? That you turned him down?' She shook her head. 'Cassie, I thought you were in love with him.'

Cass was sure she was going mad. She said, 'There was never any question of marriage.'

'There was every question,' Marcia almost howled, propelling her bodily into the drawing room. 'My God, you don't think Rohan would have involved me, if all he'd wanted had been a quick lay, do you?' She faced Cass stormily. 'Of course he wants to marry you. Why the hell do you imagine he set this whole thing up in the first place, if he wasn't crazy about you? Christ, he even took you to the cottage—his Holiest of Holies. Apart from Mother and I, no other woman's ever set foot in the place. It's always been his refuge—his sanctuary. He said he had to take you away somewhere where you could be completely alone together so he could persuade you to trust him, to believe that he could make you happy. He said you'd had a lousy marriage the first time around, and he had to prove to you somehow that he loved you, and wanted to make up to you for everything that had happened in the past.'

Cass's legs would no longer support her. She sank down on to a chair. She said tonelessly, 'He said—that?'

'Yes—and more.' Marcia gave her a look of burning reproach. 'So what went wrong? I expected you both to show up here engaged.'

Cass bit her lip. 'Perhaps he changed his mind. He never—mentioned marriage.'

'Perhaps you didn't give him time,' Marcia countered levelly.

There was a long silence, then Marcia sighed. 'I could do with a drink,' she said. 'I don't care if it is only just after breakfast. And I think you should have one too,' she added. 'You look as if you could do with it. Have you eaten this morning?'

Cass shook her head desolately. 'I'd planned to make breakfast for us both, but then I got to thinking, and it seemed better to—get out, while the going was good.'

'Instead of waiting for Rohan to wake up, and hear what he had to say on the subject,' Marcia said heavily, and sighed. 'I see. Without wishing to pry, do I infer that you and Rohan spent the night together?'

Cass flushed faintly. 'Yes.'

'Well, there's no need to be embarrassed.' Marcia's face relaxed into a smile. 'Rohan made a lot of virtuous statements about not rushing you into anything, but I guessed he'd sweep you off your feet, and into bed with him, given half a chance. You're both consenting adults, so what's the problem.' Her smile widened. 'Except that he seems to have fallen asleep before he could get round to proposing marriage. Maybe he thought you'd wake up so bemused with love that you'd agree to anything he suggested.'

Cass stared down at her hands, clenched together in her lap. 'He wasn't far wrong,' she admitted. 'Walking out was the hardest thing I've ever done in my life.' She squared her shoulders. 'But I thought I was walking out on an affair, and I knew I couldn't cope with that. So, I felt I had to leave.'

'It must have taken guts,' Marcia said idly. 'Almost as much guts as it's going to take to go back there and face him. But let's look on the bright side, and say he hasn't woken up and missed you yet.'

Cass's face was stark. 'I—can't.'

'You love him don't you?' Marcia asked unanswerably. 'Right, then you have to. You have no choice, for Rohan's sake as well as your own.'

Cass said half to herself, 'But why should he want to marry me?'

'Temporary insanity,' Marcia suggested brightly. 'I recommend you take the point up with him, rather than me.'

Cass bit her lip. 'If he still wants to talk to me,' she said helplessly. 'I did rather burn my boats.'

Marcia shrugged. 'All you can do is try,' she said. 'We won't have that drink. I'll get dressed and drive you over to the cottage.' She paused. 'I was going to suggest you took Jodie with you, but maybe she'd better stay here—until you see how the land lies.'

'No, I'd rather she went with me.' Cass gave a small, wintry smile. 'After all, it's her life too.'

And my happiness for all eternity, she thought, apprehension twisting within her. Oh God, don't let me have ruined everything.

CHAPTER ELEVEN

IT seemed a very long time before her case and Jodie's were loaded into Marcia's car, and Cass was on edge as the vehicle eventually moved off.

Jodie had stopped crying, but her mood was subdued, her large eyes anxious, and Cass felt her heart contract as she turned to give her a smile she hoped was reassuring.

She remembered what Rohan had said about Jodie picking up vibrations from her for good or ill, and strove to present an attitude of calm normality, but it wasn't easy, even with Marcia's fluent assistance.

As they neared the cottage, Cass felt her nails curling into her palms with tension.

Marcia sent her a faint smile. 'Chin up,' she advised softly. 'Remember, I'd really like to have you as a sister-in-law, Cassie, and don't let me down.'

But any hopes about Marcia's confident prophecy that Rohan would still be sleeping were soon dashed. As Marcia drove up the track towards the cottage, Cass could see him standing beside his own car.

He turned, when he heard the car, but he made no attempt to smile or come forward in welcome, and Cass felt chilled as she helped Jodie to scramble out.

Marcia deposited their cases beside them with more haste than grace.

'I think I'll push off,' she said in an undertone. 'Rohan in this mood brings out all the coward in me. Good luck.'

Cass walked forward slowly, her eyes fixed on his grim face. When they were a few yards apart, Jodie detached herself with ease from her mother and ran forward.

'Rohan,' she said stretching out her arms imperiously, and his face softened a little as he bent, swinging her up into his arms.

'Hello, sweetheart.'

'Mummy didn't believe me,' Jodie announced. 'She thought I was making up stories, when I said you were going to marry us.'

'And you managed to convince her?' Rohan kissed the tip of her nose. 'Then you're cleverer than I am.'

The irony in his voice was lost on the child, but it made Cass wince.

Jodie was wriggling, looking round her. 'Can I go and explore? Rohan—may I? It's a pretty house.'

'Yes, off you go.' He lowered her to ground level. 'Mind how you go on the stairs,' he cautioned.

As she scampered off, he turned back to Cass.

'So you came back,' he said bleakly. 'That was not the impression your note gave.'

She moistened dry lips with the tip of her tongue. 'I know, and I'm sorry, but I didn't realise . . .'

'That my intentions were honourable,' he broke in almost contemptuously. 'Well, I can understand that. Trust has never featured very prominently in our relationship to date. But I was fool enough to think that last night might have changed all that. I imagined that the fact you'd actually given yourself to me really meant something.'

She swallowed miserably, 'It did.'

'Really?' he came back at her implacably. 'So what did it mean, Cass? That you found having sex with me sufficiently bearable to tempt you to do your best for Jodie—to provide her with the kind of security, the kind of upbringing she deserves?'

He paused, the hazel eyes fixed remorselessly on her pale face, and quivering lips.

Then he said, more gently, 'I love Jodie. I wish that she was my child. I wish I'd put the seed she grew from into your body. I wish I'd been there with you when she was born. But I'm not prepared to be married for her sake only, Cassandra. I'm selfish enough to need my wife to want me for myself, as I want and love her. Not because I'm a suitable father-figure for her daughter.' He paused again. 'If she hadn't persuaded you, would you have come back, I wonder?'

She said in a low voice, 'It was because of her that I left. If it had been myself alone, I'd have stayed with you, Rohan, for as long as you wanted, been anything to you that you wanted. I—I didn't expect marriage. You could have anyone, after all.'

'I've spoken to you before about being humble,' he said grimly. 'So, what did you think I wanted from you. A quick sexual romp?' He shook his head slowly. 'Cassie, what happened for us last night was a miracle, and God knows I never expected it. Feeling as you did, I'd expected it to take months for us to reach anything approaching that kind of rapport. Years even.' He sighed. 'I took you last night because it seemed to me that going to bed with me had become some kind of obstacle for you. An emotional hurdle that we needed to get across together. I thought once that "first time" with all its connotations was behind us, we'd have something to build on. And then—suddenly— there was Paradise. I thought it was mutual. When I woke this morning and found you gone, I didn't believe it. Why did you go?'

'Because I couldn't bear to see you walk away from me eventually or, worse still, hang around out of a sense of—of compassion.' A slow scalding tear trickled down her cheek. 'It seemed to me that if I stayed, I was only piling up heartbreak for myself—and for Jodie, who'd have started loving you and relying on you more and more, the longer it went on.'

'So you decided to break my heart instead.' Rohan smiled faintly. 'Cassie, did you really think I was so starved of female companionship that I needed to go to those lengths to win you, if all I wanted was a few weeks' sex?'

Colour rose in her face. 'You never mentioned—caring for me.'

'I was afraid of frightening you still further,' he said ruefully. 'And don't forget you've been spitting at me like an angry cat ever since we met. I had no real reason to believe that you'd be prepared to listen to any kind of declaration from me.' He slanted a sardonic look at her. 'If I'd gone down on one knee and proposed to you when I first brought you here, would you have fallen into my arms with delight? Or would you have kicked me in the teeth and walked out?'

'Probably that,' she mumbled.

'Exactly,' Rohan said drily. 'Which is basically why I said nothing. I thought it was best to let you get used to me first, even enjoy being with me, before I started talking about a permanent thing like marriage.' He threw his head back and looked at her. 'Because in my family, Cassandra, marriage is for life. We don't give up easily.'

'As you've already demonstrated,' Cass said, with something of her old fire. 'Wasn't there something about "Escape me? Never" even that first day at Finiston Webber?'

'There was,' he said levelly. 'You ran into my arms, and it was like electricity. I thought—an advanced case of instant sexual chemistry, and proceeded accordingly. But it wasn't until the next day when I came to the flat and found you in bed with 'flu that I realised what was really going on.' He smiled reminiscently. 'You were ill and peevish, and by no means the delectable woman I'd fancied so avidly the day before, and yet I couldn't tear myself away. I straightened your bed, and gave you a drink and just sat there watching you. And I thought, "That's my wife." It was that simple. The problems began when I tried persuading you.'

'That simple?' Cass's brows lifted. 'Are you forgetting Serena Vance?'

His smile became a grin. 'I don't wear my heart on my sleeve, Cassandra. If you thought for one minute, I was going to hang round "alone and palely loitering" while you did your *Belle*

Dame sans Merci act all over London, then you could think again. And Serena was—there. Very convenient. But that's all she was.'

She was still uncertain. 'But you brought her here, and Marcia was positive you'd never asked anyone to the cottage but me.'

He frowned slightly. 'Marcia's right.'

'But you told me when I asked that she thought the place was quaint,' she pointed out with a pang.

'So she did,' he said casually. 'She was at Graystocks once, having turned up uninvited I may add, when I was showing Marcia some before and after photographs I'd taken of the cottage. Serena never misses out on an opportunity to gush,' he added caustically. 'But I wouldn't have had her within a hundred miles of the place. This is my home, Cassandra. The place I intend to share with the woman I love.' He paused, almost uncertainly. 'If that's what she wants too, of course. You may not want to be stranded with me in this backwater on a permanent basis. You've got a career, after all.'

'For the time being, I have.' She began to smile again, the glow of love and desire irradiating her entire being. 'But I'll be happy to retire here when those brothers and sisters you've been planning with Jodie start coming along.'

He said gently, 'Tell me you love me, Cassandra. Let me hear the words. You've given me a bad time too, remember.'

She looked at him with her heart in her eyes, 'I love you, Rohan. Too much, I think.'

'It can never be that.' He came to her then, at last, his arms going round her, drawing her against him. She registered wonderingly that he was trembling. He whispered, 'You have a hell of a way to go to catch up with me, darling.' He bent and kissed her mouth with heart-stopping tenderness, and the beginning of passion. When he lifted his head, he said unevenly, 'You'll never know what I went through this morning when I reached for you, and you weren't there. That isn't going to happen again.'

She bit her lip. 'Rohan, I can't sleep with you. What will Jodie think?'

'Leave Jodie to me,' he said. 'Anyway, she'll be too busy hatching up this bridesmaid's dress with Marcia to worry about what we're up to.' He paused. 'My mother and father get back from their trip in a fortnight. I thought we'd get married then.'

She said uneasily, 'And how are they going to react to you marrying a widow with a child?'

'With enthusiam, when I talked to them about it on the telephone,' he said. 'I told them I adored you, and that Jodie was a bonus.'

The bonus chose that moment to come flying out of the house.

'I love your house,' she announced, inveigling herself between them with the air of one who has the right. 'I'd like the littlest bedroom to be mine, only someone else is using it.'

'No, they're not,' Rohan told her. 'Your mother's decided to sleep in my room from now on, so it's all yours.'

Jodie drew a deep breath, and looked up at them, her face unclouded. 'Just like a real Mummy and Daddy?' she demanded.

Rohan ruffled her hair. 'Exactly like that, madam.'

'Oh.' The breath she drew seemed composed of sheer ecstasy. The gaze she turned on her future stepfather was angelically beguiling. 'And I've seen a wonderful place for the swing.'

Cass began to shake with laughter. 'Darling,' she said. 'Are you sure you know what you're taking on?'

'Quite sure,' Rohan said, and the words sounded like a vow. He picked Jodie up and settled her on his hip, then slid an arm round Cass and began to walk with them both towards the front door. 'Now, let's go home.'

Coming Next Month

879 THAI TRIANGLE Jayne Bauling
In Thailand an artist tries to bring two brothers together before it's too late. In love with one, she can't break her promise to the other—not even to avoid heartache.

880 PILLOW PORTRAITS Rosemary Carter
An assignment to ghostwrite a famous artist's autobiography seems like the chance of a lifetime—until he insists on her baring her soul, too, even her deepest secret.

881 DARK DREAM Daphne Clair
When her childhood sweetheart brings home a fiancée, a young woman finds herself marrying a widower who claims to love her. Yet he still dreams about his first wife!

882 POINT OF IMPACT Emma Darcy
On a ferry in Sydney Harbour it is a night to celebrate. Although the man she once loved is present, a model throws caution to the wind and announces her engagement. The shockwaves are immediate!

883 INJURED INNOCENT Penny Jordan
Co-guardians are at loggerheads—not so much over their differing views on how to raise the little girls as over an unresolved conflict from the past.

884 DANGER ZONE Madeleine Ker
An English fashion designer in New York is drawn to a successful merchant banker, despite his disturbing, reckless streak and the strain it places on their love.

885 SWEET AS MY REVENGE Susan Napier
The owner of an Australian secretarial agency is trapped and forced to face the consequences of her foolhardy act to save her brother's career. But no one tricks her into falling in love.

886 ICE INTO FIRE Lilian Peake
When her parents' marriage shatters, a young woman vows never to be burned by love. But at a Swiss chalet, a man who equally mistrusts emotion manages to melt her resolve.

Available in May wherever paperback books are sold, or through Harlequin Reader Service.

In the U.S.
P.O. Box 1397
Buffalo, N.Y.
14240-1397

In Canada
P.O. Box 2800, Postal Station A
5170 Yonge Street
Willowdale, Ontario M2N 6J3

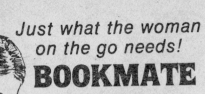

Take
4 novels
and a
surprise gift
FREE